Virginie has been caring for her mentally ill mother practically since she could walk. When brilliant, hard-working Virginie meets carefree, happy-go-lucky Felix at university, they fall madly in love. This should be a wonderful, liberating experience for the women, but when Virginie learns the local nationalist party are conspiring to use her mother to infiltrate their council, she resolves to put a stop to their subterfuge.

When Virginie's mother is found dead, Virginie is arrested and charged with her murder. She must go to trial and fight a battle for her life. Virginie knows just how to save herself, but she needs someone reliable on the outside to carry out her plans. Can Felix finally grow up and do what is needed to save the woman of her dreams from the death penalty…?

AN ALEX SPEAR NOVEL

Other published works from Alex Spear

People Person
Out

Dedication

My thanks go to Frances, who read this one first.

This book is for my brother, who gave me my pen-name;
my sister, whose name I gave her;
my dad, whose name I had first;
my wife, whose name I took;
and for my mum, who taught me the names of everything in the world and whose passion and beauty will last till the end of time.
I love you all.

ALEX SPEAR

RESTRAINT

Published by:
Shadoe Publishing
Copyright © September 2018 by Alex Spear

ISBN-13: 978-1727447408
ISBN-10: 1727447409

Copyright © September 2018 by Alex Spear

All rights reserved. No part of this book may be reproduced, stored in a retrieval system or transmitted in any form or by any means without the prior written permission of Alex Spear or Shadoe Publishing, except by a reviewer who may quote brief passages in a review to be printed in a newspaper, magazine, or journal.

Alex Spear is available for comments at alex.spear@live.co.uk as well as on Facebook @ https://www.facebook.com/alexspearbooks/ or on Twitter @alexspearwriter, on LinkedIn @ Alex Spear if you would like to follow to find out about stories and books releases or check with www. ShadoePublishing.com or http://ShadoePublishing.wordpress.com/.

www.shadoepublishing.com

ShadoePublishing@gmail.com

Shadoe Publishing is a United States of America company

Edited by: Deb Amia, Grammar Queen grammarqueen.com
Cover by: K'Anne Meinel @ Shadoe Publishing

PEOPLE PERSON

PUBLISHER'S NOTE

This is a work of fiction. Names, characters, places, and incidents are the product of the author's imagination or are used fictitiously, and any resemblance to actual persons, living or dead, business establishments, events, or locales is entirely coincidental.

The publisher does not have any control over and does not assume any responsibility for author or third-party Web sites or their content.

PEOPLE PERSON

Part One

The defence of loss of control.

Like provocation, if loss of control can be proven, it serves as a partial defence to murder, reducing a conviction of murder to manslaughter.

Someone who kills may be convicted of manslaughter rather than murder if:

- the defendant's acts and omissions in doing or being a party to the killing resulted from their loss of self-control;
- the loss of self-control had a qualifying trigger including a justifiable sense of feeling wronged;
- and a person of the defendant's sex and age with a normal degree of tolerance and self-restraint and in the circumstances of the defendant might have reacted in the same way to the defendant.

There is no requirement that the loss of self-control be sudden.

Whether a person of the defendant's sex and age with a normal degree of tolerance and self-restraint and in the circumstances of the defendant might have reacted in the same way is a question for the jury to decide.

Section 54 of the Criminal Justice Act 2009

Those who can make you believe absurdities can make you commit atrocities.
Voltaire
1694 – 1778

PEOPLE PERSON

Chapter One

"No, I've not done it before—not this way round, anyway." Raucous laughter. She sounded like she bit the filters off fifty Benson and Hedges a day. She edged her way through the rows of chairs to where we sat.

My legs bouncing up and down did very little to dissipate my anxiety. Irene (purple hair) and I watched as she shimmied up to us, though Irene did not pause for breath as she shared with me the pros and cons of going *now* to get her SmartCard from the canteen or waiting till a bit *later*. I couldn't even think about eating, and for me that's serious. I could have cheered when the enormous bailiff strode to the front and clapped his hands.

"New jurors. Any new jurors there?" he boomed. "Take a seat please. Short video."

He had some difficulty getting it to play, which gave her enough time to settle herself down next to me and say, "I'm Rita, dears. Last time I was here was with my son. They gave him six months, and I said to myself—"

"Ah, it's working," intoned the bailiff.

The lights went down, and we were silent. I stared at the screen, not seeing a thing. I was gripping my hands together so tightly I had faint pins and needles in my fingers.

Afterwards, Rita said, "Well, that was a laugh a minute, wasn't it?" and rasped with laughter. "Your decision affects lives! Gawd help us all."

"And other trials," said Irene.

"That's right." Rita looked pleased about this one. She nodded and said it again, "That's right." She nudged me with a skinny elbow. "We'll have to put our black hats on, won't we, girls?"

At length, Irene said she thought she would take her chance to nip to the canteen, which was at one end of the large room. We could just hear her over the scrape of chairs saying, "Oh, no. Sorry, you've got me down under my married name."

I walked away to an empty table, sat down, and pulled out my book. I tried to read. The print blurred before my eyes, but I was desperate for an excuse not to talk.

Rita strolled up and pulled out a chair. "You don't mind if I join you, do you, dears?" she crooned, then unpacked her large handbag.

I put my book away when the photos came out. "This is my youngest grandson in his cadet uniform," she was saying. She held the photos before her in a fan, like cards, and I went through the motions of looking at them with her. "This is his dad; he's in Iraq now." She seemed to have gold rings on every finger. Her hands were impressively wrinkled.

Irene came to our table and smiled hesitantly. Rita indicated that she was to sit down and admire the photos also. "They've finished that extension now. It's a twenty-five-metre swimming pool. I said to them, "There's no sense in having all that garden. Get yourself a pool while the children are still young enough to enjoy it.""

Irene commented and asked some of the questions you're supposed to ask about other people's photos. "How old is he? He's tall like his dad. Isn't she pretty! Was she the little flower girl in that one?"

The bailiff reappeared, and we were called down with another nine people. We sat in a waiting room that made you think of all you'd done wrong in your life and how you would be judged. We were men and women, young and old, and we did not speak to each other. The others might naturally feel guilty in that environment, but it was probable that I was the only one fighting down a secret of this magnitude. Even my bones seemed to hum with anxiety.

The bailiff came among us to inquire individually whether we were in any way connected with the trial and whether we knew anything at

PEOPLE PERSON

all that might influence our view or sway us towards cruelty or compassion for the woman involved. To mislead the Crown on this point would be a very serious matter. When he asked me, I found that lying was harder than I had imagined but managed to croak, "I swear I don't know her."

We were led into the courtroom, and as we sat down in rows, one by one we were sworn in. Craning my neck to the side, I saw her.

She was sitting behind a transparent screen at the back of the courtroom. Laughably, she had been assigned a burly policeman to sit on each side of her. She had her hands neatly folded in her lap. Her close-cropped hair was slightly tousled, as if her sleep had been troubled, and she seemed even thinner than I remembered. Very thin but not fragile—filled with quiet purpose. Her calm, steady gaze was not directed at me.

As the judge told us to sit down, Rita hissed in my ear, "She doesn't look the bloodthirsty type, does she? Looks more like a schoolmarm!" before the bailiff raised a finger at her to be quiet.

My legs were trembling. I felt faint and had to hold on to the wooden shelf in front of me. Virginie stood to confirm her name and her respectable, suburban address. She would be pleading not guilty to murder but would demonstrate that it was a case of manslaughter due to loss of control and provocation. Her solicitor looked as if he would eat her alive when she said this, and a vein stood out dangerously in his neck.

With a start, I wondered who was tending her beautiful garden.

ALEX SPEAR

PEOPLE PERSON

Chapter Two

Blissful rest, with dreams of straight lines, neatly filed experiences, tiny labels in exquisite handwriting—copperplate in black ink on tiny, crisp white rectangles.

It couldn't last.

Sudden punch of light and noise and confusion –

"Get up, Virginie! It's ten to eight! You can eat in the car! Hugo's waiting!"

Virginie leapt up, every muscle cocked, wrenched from sleep by the explosion of Medusa. Medusa was shedding curlers, framed in the doorway, bringing in her aura of inefficient noise and pointless activity and leaving behind her a trail of chaos. She hurricaned away and her noise ebbed a little, though she could still be heard rumbling in the distance.

Virginie breathed. She was propped up on her hands, mummified in mismatched, shredded, and stained blankets. Her quiet, reasonable mind recoiled from the room around her.

As always, she could not decide what to do first. Her brain was the champion of order, clarity, and logic, but it shrank back in horror from her situation and became subdued … each morning, a little more.

She looked around her tiny bedroom. The floor was not visible. Possessions were everywhere: clothes, books, and furniture coming up to the height of the bed and covering all the available space. Every time Virginie spent a weekend of labour tidying her room and got it down to floor level, Medusa seized upon the space and piled in her own possessions. If no junk was available in the house, Medusa would go and collect more from jumble sales and the cheapest kind of charity shop, which resembled her home.

Virginie wished again she were allowed an alarm clock. She hated waking up late and this panicky feeling that she had no time to order her thoughts.

She wanted to dress. Her mind never stopped imagining a clean, ironed school uniform to step into, no matter how cruel such a thought was. She scanned the debris for items of clothing. In her mind's eye she could see herself beaming as she buttoned a starched, white shirt in front of a clean, unbroken mirror. She looked around the room packed with rubbish. She spotted yesterday's shirt near the door. It had fallen off the hanger, probably from when Medusa had crashed in.

Virginie gingerly placed a foot on a thinner area of the pile of debris beside the bed. So far, so good. Only a few creaking, breaking sounds underfoot, and she was able to surf the rubbish and exit her bedroom. She squeezed around the dead wicker sofa that slumped against the door. The junk in the doorway meant Virginie could not close her bedroom door, meaning any phone conversation she had would be clearly audible and monitored by the Medusa, who tended to materialise in another upstairs room on the rare occasion Virginie made or received a call.

Virginie grabbed the shirt and inched her way down the stairs, past teetering piles of faded clothing and chipped tea sets that were forty years old and had been hideous even when new.

Medusa was frantically piling rubbish into the porch to take to the car. Every morning she filled her small car with detritus—papers, plastic bags, coat hangers, plant pots—and every evening she brought it all home again. Time-consuming, pointless, and mad.

"Mum, where's my tie and skirt?" Virginie asked.

"Oh, I don't know, child," she puffed, piling more papers onto the doormat. "Go and look in the kitchen. There might be some clean clothes in a pile somewhere."

Virginie stepped carefully over her mother's makeshift bed, a mattress in the middle of the living room floor. The Medusa would tell shocked visitors that she slept on the sitting room floor for the good of

PEOPLE PERSON

her back, but the truth was there wasn't a single bedroom with enough space in it for a bed. Every available inch of the house was used as storage space, given over to the junk, so the people had to pack themselves away in boxes. But visitors came rarely and never twice.

For Virginie, living in this rat's nest was painful and humiliating. She felt reluctant to make friends with the other children in her class at school in case they wanted to come home for tea. She couldn't bear anyone outside the family knowing that she lived like this. The stress of her secret kept her alone and silent.

Virginie managed to find all the items of school uniform she needed except for a school tie. Glancing at the kitchen clock, which was always seven hours forty-three minutes slow, she realized she had a choice between going without a tie or being late for school and possibly still not being able to locate a tie. She sighed as she realized she would have to go to school without the full uniform again. She reflected that last week had been worse when she had not been able to lay hands on a school skirt and she had to wear an old pair of her mother's culottes.

Virginie quickly got dressed in the downstairs toilet, standing on a heap of loo rolls, and hurried to the car. Hugo was sitting in his booster seat in his long nightshirt, gurgling and eating toast. He had a marmite and dribble ring around his rosebud lips.

Of course, Medusa was a made-up name. Virginie had mentally christened her mother 'the Medusa' some years before for two reasons. The first was that her hair was always twisted into curlers, which bobbed and threatened to escape, especially when she was animated, which was most of the time. The second was that she had a peculiar control over Virginie, who would attempt to assert herself and stand up for a little independence, a little choice about how she lived her life but would be utterly defeated by her mother. Her mother would fix her with an unquestionable stare while she noisily explained that whatever Virginie was suggesting was silly, unnecessary, or insulting. Virginie would feel near enough turned to stone, paralyzed by her mother's force and unable to fight back.

Virginie was seven. She had lived long enough to have taken control in other invisible ways. One thing she controlled was the food she put in her mouth. Medusa could listen to her phone calls, stop her from having friends, make her late for school, and make her feel like her chest was going to explode with the anger, the resentment, and the stress, but she could not control how she ate.

Virginie had taken a slice of bread from the kitchen. Sitting in the car, Virginie waited fretfully for her mother to come out of the house and drive her to school. Her stomach growled with early-morning hunger. She started her ritual of eating the bread as slowly as she could, nibbling tiny bites all along one side and seeing how straight a line she could create. She would be furious with herself if the line seemed to curve or was at an angle to the opposite crust.

She had begun this private defiance of eating very slowly and carefully from the age of five or six. Recently, she had progressed to the precision of cutting the messy, hearty food into regular shapes: squares, triangles, and hexagons. Sometimes, for variety, she would eat food in strict alphabetical order or in stages dictated by colour or density.

Hugo gurgled and waved a pudgy hand. Virginie bounced up and down on the seat, staring at the clock on the dashboard—8:13. She wished again and again that she had her own alarm clock, so she could prepare herself and maybe even help her mother get ready, so they had a chance of leaving the house on time. Beside Virginie's bed lay three alarm clocks, all broken. Virginie wanted to throw them all away and buy one from Argos, one that really worked. She had looked in the catalogue, and the cheapest one was less than three pounds.

But Medusa always said that she could fix the red one, and there's nothing wrong with the white one; it just needs new batteries. Virginie would ask hesitantly whether it would be OK if she had some new batteries then, and Medusa would present her with an ice cream box full of batteries. Some were bubbled and studded, some were green, some hissed faintly, and some gave off a powerful odor, which could cause hallucinations. Virginie had calculated and concluded that testing the alarm clock with all possible combinations of two batteries, at a rate of one every minute, would take most of a day. She never had that kind of time to herself. She went to school, then she came home and did her homework cross-legged on her bed.

She knew she loved girls, but there would be time for that later in her life. Her duty now was clear.

At the weekends, she did her best to organise the house, and she laboured on the wild back garden. Medusa did not like to come into the garden, so it became a wonderful sanctuary. These were the hours of the week Virginie was happiest: digging and weeding, creating orderly beds out of the chaos of nature, planting some old seeds she found in a

PEOPLE PERSON

packet in the tool shed, and watching week by week as the green shoots started to appear.

The thought of the garden was her touchstone. Through a quiet meditation on her oasis of plants, stones, and perfect, little insects, Virginie could calm her mind when it otherwise seemed impossible. Sitting in the car, fighting down the urge to beep the horn, she remembered one long, sunny afternoon she had spent in her garden. She remembered how she had watched in fascination as a harvest spider had spun its web across two wild bushes that framed the crazy path. The spider had spent two hours creating a shimmering, geometrically perfect web of about a square metre in size. Virginie felt that both she and the spider had admired it together from their separate vantage points ... until Medusa had appeared from nowhere on a pointless errand. She had sailed straight through the web, sending the spider flying and accidentally stepping on Virginie's green shoots in the flower bed.

"I came out for the washing. Where's it gone?" Medusa asked with genuine confusion.

"You haven't done any washing today, Mummy," Virginie explained, the concern in her voice just audible. Did her mum really not know? But she told herself to be strong for them both, however scary it felt. "Go back inside. It's quite cold out here. I'll come and make you a cup of tea in a minute."

Medusa flopped on the stone steps outside their house. "Tell me one of your stories, Virginie," she crooned, sounding melancholy. "You have a fine mind, and your stories always lift me."

Virginie obediently repeated the story she often thought of as she fell asleep.

"Once there was a girl who could only tell the truth. She and her brother were imprisoned in a horrible, ruined old castle by an evil witch and a mad old wizard. The wizard taught the girl how to make potions, but then, he died. The witch was strangely controlled by an evil king in the area. The girl fell in love with a lazy prince. The girl saved herself by killing the witch. Then the girl was imprisoned again and tormented by a monster, who was really a beautiful mother under a curse. And the girl carried on telling the truth even though she was imprisoned. She was slandered, and the prince that she loved heard and believed that she had been untrue. But she managed to break the spell and turn the monster back into the beautiful mother she had been and set the other prisoners free in their hearts. Then, she escaped from the prison and returned home."

Medusa always smiled and repeated the final words. "She escaped from the prison and returned home."

Virginie had watched as the spider tirelessly began to spin its web again from scratch. Standing up to go inside, she had brushed away a tear, angry with herself for letting her distress get the better of her.

PEOPLE PERSON

Chapter Three

The case for the prosecution was not as aggressive as some cases. The barrister stood up and tilted her head to one side to indicate compassion as she addressed the jury. She said in hushed tones that she recognized this was a terribly *sensitive* matter, one that many would feel was private within the family, but nevertheless she knew the jurors were intelligent and would understand that assisted suicide was still against the law in this country. Although a family member suffering from a progressive illness was very distressing, the law was in place to protect elderly people from being encouraged to end their own lives early simply because those around them found them troublesome.

As the barrister went on, I felt a restlessness grow among the jurors around me. I glanced from side to side. Rita was virtually hissing her disapproval. A young man on the other side of me was shaking his head angrily and seemed hardly able to stand listening to this point of view.

The barrister sat down. The counsel for the defence said tersely that the jury were not being asked to believe that it was a defence of assisted suicide but that his client had been honest about her part in a case of manslaughter for reasons of ongoing provocation. He had no further comments at this time other than to remind the jury that Virginie had co-operated with the police from the arrest onwards, and her conduct in Holloway while on remand had been so exemplary that it had been remarked upon by virtually everyone that had encountered her. He didn't glance at his client.

I looked at Virginie, trying not to catch her eye. She was certainly listening to the proceedings but without anxiety. My knees had begun to bounce again, up and down, up and down, until I realized I was causing the wooden bench to vibrate, and Rita gave me a look.

The first witness was a neighbour, Mr. Patel from several doors down, who had lent a hand with the rebuilding of the front wall. He said that Virginie's mother, Mrs. Harper, had been popular and well-respected locally. Of course, people had known that both she and her father had been eccentric. The house had seemed somewhat chaotic. But she had been a pillar of the community, involved with so many associations and projects that it was an impossible suggestion that she had been unable to cope. She had certainly not been frail physically.

With a small start, I realized that Reginald Pathaway, the local representative of the Keeping Britain Great Party, was sitting in the public gallery. He was watching the trial with grim purpose and was making notes of what was being said.

The counsel for the prosecution asked Mr. Patel whether, in his opinion, Virginie's mother had appeared to be in despair. The answer was no. Had she expressed a weariness with life and the condition she was suffering from? Had she perhaps said that she was experiencing such intense pain that her quality of life was minimal? Mr. Patel said this was not the case and he had never heard Mrs. Harper say this.

The counsel for the prosecution walked slowly around the small table on which she had spread out her notes. She stood in front of the jury, sat back on the edge of the table, and took her time to look at each one of us carefully. I managed to hold her gaze when she turned it on me. As she looked away, I breathed. She did not have the same formidable quality to her eye contact that Virginie had. That power must come from a life of integrity.

The solicitor's eyes momentarily cast down and she loudly asked the witness, "Do you believe that this woman, this mother and community leader, Mathilde Harper, wanted to die?"

"No, I do not. However, apparently, her daughter wished her dead," Mr. Patel said with an apologetic glance at Virginie.

"Conjecture, Your Honour," muttered Virginie's solicitor.

PEOPLE PERSON

I looked to the back of the court. Virginie's eyes were blazing, and I fell in love all over again. She fixed that incredible laser beam stare on the prosecuting solicitor who, walking back to her seat, caught her eye and was almost abashed but not quite. Virginie was perfectly still yet somehow conveyed boundless energy.

I sat on my hands and forced myself to let the trial unfold.

"Objection overruled," declared the judge primly. "The lady in question is dead, and the defendant does not deny that she was the cause. Now, can we get on?"

ALEX SPEAR

PEOPLE PERSON

Chapter Four

The bell had already been rung as Virginie ran into the playground, and the children were already in judgmental lines while registers were called. Virginie could not stop her brain from repeating, "Always late. I am always late."

She spotted her class and slipped to the end of the line, hoping Miss Long would think she had been there all along. She also hoped Miss Long would not notice her lack of tie. The children nearest her noticed, as always.

"Where's your tie?"

"How come you're always the last to get to school?"

"Why haven't you got a tie on?"

"Virginie Harper," called Miss Long.

She looked up guiltily.

Miss Long smiled kindly. "Not quite late, my dear," the teacher lied and marked her in.

School for Virginie was an ordered, spacious place. She found the rules calming. The people around her could be depended upon and would not suddenly explode with unpredictable, bizarre behavior. If children were disorganized, they would usually be shown how to rearrange themselves and achieve the peace of self-discipline. The other children liked Virginie and wanted to get to know her, but she preferred her own company and was quiet apart from when she saw an injustice. In the face of a bully, she could become quite forceful.

There was a big, angry girl called Deidre. She hated boys and always wanted to fight them in the playground. At playtime that morning, she was picking on timid William, who was often teased because of his religion.

"Why can't you do ICT class?" Deidre demanded of William, who was sitting on the floor playing marbles by himself.

Virginie, contemplating the trees nearby, was puzzled. Everyone knew that William couldn't do ICT class because his family didn't believe in computers; there had been a special assembly about it.

"Is it because you're too thick?" Deidre stooped to yell in William's face. He tried to ignore her. Her huge shadow fell across him, and the other children realized with glee that there was going to be a punch up. "Oi, I'm talking to you," shouted Deidre and gave him a shove.

"That's not fair," piped up a small, clear voice. The shocked intake of breath from all directions caused both Deidre and William to whirl round. Virginie was glaring up at Deidre with her enormous, outraged eyes.

Deidre lumbered over to Virginie and gave her a mighty cuff round the head. Virginie staggered but remained on her feet. She tasted blood and put her hand to her lip. Deidre laughed and seemed about to hit Virginie again.

Virginie considered her options. Option one: run and tell a teacher, but this would leave William alone with Deidre, and he could be a bloody pulp by the time she got back. Option two: hit Deidre back, but Deidre was enormous and would probably hardly feel any punch Virginie could muster. Option three: use reason to defeat brutality.

"Why are you always so angry with everyone?" Virginie asked at the top of her voice. "You were having a go at Femi yesterday and she hadn't done anything to you."

Femi, playing nearby with a skipping rope, stopped and looked over.

Virginie continued, "Today, it's William. Who will it be tomorrow? Why don't you stop being so cross with everyone?"

Deidre looked baffled. She kicked the floor near William, and he scrambled backwards away from her. She was looking around, red in the face, blustering, angry, and embarrassed. Lots of children near

PEOPLE PERSON

them had heard Virginie. Girls and boys had stopped what they were doing and were listening, watching.

"Why don't you just be nice?" concluded Virginie. "I'd play with you, if you wanted."

"I don't want to play with you, little shit," shouted Deidre and threw a half-hearted punch at Virginie, which didn't connect. But there was an audience now, and some of the older children shouted, "Don't hit her," although at least one was chanting, "Fight, fight." Deidre appeared to be confused, less determined to attack either William or Virginie. She turned on her heel and stomped off.

William seemed too downtrodden to feel grateful for this heroism. He carried on with his marbles, head down. But Femi seemed impressed by the tiny girl who had managed to get the bully to go away, even temporarily. She came up to Virginie and asked her if she'd like to play at skipping for a bit.

Virginie thought she would, this once, instead of just sitting under a tree thinking her own thoughts. She joined Femi and some of the other girls and they twirled the rope for her to jump over. For once, she didn't notice that they all wore pretty, little, lacy ankle socks and matching black patent shoes. She concentrated so hard on jumping over the rope and not letting it knock against her ankles that for a while, she forgot to be embarrassed that she was wearing odd socks and a pair of her mother's sandals, her own shoes being lost somewhere in the house.

At the end of the day, Virginie hopped up and down at the school gates as the other children were gradually collected by neat parents and childminders in tidy cars. Her mother was the last to arrive, as ever.

When the Medusa eventually pulled up, Virginie opened the car door and shoved a load of books, papers, and tins off the seats and into the middle, so she could get in and sit down. There was even more clutter under her feet, and she tried her best not to break anything. She sternly reminded herself again to stay slim and light as this made it easier to tread gently on her mother's possessions.

They began their evening interaction. Medusa insisted on Virginie recounting every moment of her day: every lesson, every bite of lunch, every conversation, every breath. Her mother was ravenously interested in every detail. Then came the Medusa's intricate tale of every second of *her* experience: every meaningful glance from another council member, every power struggle with every colleague, and an endless analysis of *what it all meant*.

As she listened, Virginie reflected once again on how mentally close she felt to her mother. She knew everything her mother thought about everything and everyone. If they were in her garden, Virginie thought she would be a sapling planted too close to an established tree, and being obstructed by it, forced to twine round it. She accidentally wandered into her own thoughts for a moment then realized with a guilty start that the Medusa was still relating some incident that had affected her deeply, thrown her emotionally off-balance, and therefore needed lengthy discussion and dissection. Virginie didn't mean to ignore her mother, whom she loved and wanted to look after, but occasionally, she really *had* to think her own thoughts and not share them.

"Are you hungry?" bellowed the Medusa and scrabbled around for a packet of Penguin biscuits she had stashed underneath the passenger seat.

"Not really. Thanks, Mum," Virginie soothed.

"But you didn't eat all your sandwich today. And I'm sure you didn't have enough breakfast." The Medusa looked at Virginie in the rear-view mirror. "Perhaps you're dehydrated?" She found an unopened bottle of lemonade left in the car from a distant shopping trip and thrust it at her daughter. "You look a bit pale. Do you feel faint? Sick?"

Medusa hadn't the adult instinct not to take childish whims too seriously. Consequently, every nuance in Virginie's moods was endlessly analyzed. Virginie was beginning to become afraid of sharing her feelings because they seemed to morph and grow at a terrifying rate under her mother's over-anxious gaze.

She hadn't felt ill until then. She tasted the lemonade and felt worse. Her tummy did feel slightly strange, or was it just her imagination? The Medusa seemed to prod open each harmless fluctuation in a child's mood until she created complications, and she encouraged hypochondria as though a child knows what is best for her. Virginie felt weary with the responsibility of being so important and yet so powerless.

PEOPLE PERSON

Chapter Five

In the room stood a huge, polished table. The blinds were down, and it was dark as well as unbearably hot. The bailiff pushed through us to get the windows open a crack. Jake sat down at the table first.

"Can we get hold of the murder weapon?" he breezed. The bailiff said we could, and bustled away to arrange this.

I had been hoping someone would suggest this, so I wouldn't have to. I sat down at the table as well and said to some members of the jury near me, "Well, what do we think then? Self-defence? A mercy killing? Euthanasia?"

Rita had been hovering by the table, looking slightly hesitant about sitting down without permission being granted by an authority figure. But at my words her face became resolute. "Murder is murder," she said and sat down with an air of finality. "And killing your own mother is just about the worst crime there is."

My heart sank. Virginie should never have flatly denied the assisted suicide suggestion. The jury had been ready to believe that one and were prepared to imagine that it had been the action of a concerned daughter. They had been on her side until she had taken the stand and cheerfully rejected each lifeline she had been offered. The police evidence had clearly demonstrated that no one would ever have known the truth, yet the defendant seemed determined not to lie, even to save her own skin.

The bailiff brought in a large, transparent, plastic tube; the police investigation packaging, which housed the stout table leg. There was a label on the side. The name of the deceased and the date she had been found dead was scribbled on it. The table leg was the item that the counsel for the prosecution had expertly argued had been used to kill Virginie's mother. Three blows to the head. Through the protective tubing we could see that the table leg had a little dried blood along one side, and a hair or two from an old woman's head still clung to it.

I had hoped I wouldn't need to create doubt in the minds of the other eleven people in that room, so I could have kissed Irene when she sat down next to me and ran her hands over the packaging of the murder weapon and said, "How on earth could that woman have lifted this?"

"Indeed, she couldn't," said an old, dignified man beside me.

Irene attempted to lift the table leg in its tube. Grasping one end as if about to attack, she raised it clumsily. She could hardly keep the thing lifted above shoulder height and had to ease it back down onto the table with a groan.

Jake was excited. "I knew we needed to see the murder weapon," he grinned. "Are you saying a woman couldn't have done it?" My heart gave a little flutter of hope. Jake picked up the weapon himself. "It's easy for me, of course," he grunted.

"Maybe she's strong," said a very young girl with a pierced lip.

"Nah, mate. Nah," insisted Jake, "a woman couldn't have swung this. And she's a tiny, little thing. Didn't you see her?"

"I saw how composed she was when she took the stand," Rita said ominously. "Made my blood run cold. Not a scrap of remorse."

Virginie had been a formidable sight when she testified, that was for sure.

I remembered the deadly hush as she had quietly walked across the courtroom and climbed up onto the small dais.

The counsel for the prosecution was an Oxford graduate called Olivia. Olivia had turned thirty-five that week. She was feeling rather old and unmarried, to tell the truth, but one thing she was very proud of was the career she had built with her courtroom manner. Olivia was careful to create the kind of little girl sex appeal that inspires protective feelings in ageing, moneyed male chests.

PEOPLE PERSON

"Ms. Harper," she began, "I understand how painful your mother's failing health must have been for you."

Olivia had realized early on in her career that she could not emulate the aggressive, barracking style of her male counterparts, so instead she employed a naïve style of questioning designed to win the hearts of the jury.

"May I ask how much pain your mother was in?"

Virginie said, "My mother was not in any physical pain."

On this morning, Olivia had memorized a list of questions for the cross-examination. She would ask them in a disingenuous, sing-song voice, as though they were just occurring to her. Judge Palmer was hanging on her every word. She hoped he would take her for a drink later. He had already complimented her on her little skirt suit, the letch.

"Your grandfather died recently, I believe. Were you still upset by this? Were you concerned for your mother, left alone without parent or husband for support? Did you, perhaps, want to spare her further heartache?"

Olivia had done her research. She understood that Virginie's grandfather had been a difficult fantasist and was unlikely to be missed by anyone, least of all his mad daughter and long-suffering granddaughter. Working on the age-old principle of never asking a question to which one does not know the answer, she was systematically poisoning any defense Virginie might hope to rely on.

"My mother was recently bereaved, yes, but she was saddened not bereft. My own judgement was not affected by my grandfather's death."

I wanted to shout, *'Too capable! Not vulnerable enough!'* Virginie was losing the jury, that much was obvious. I glanced at Rita. She was starting to look as if she were chewing a wasp.

Olivia maintained her earnest woman-to-woman tone. "Had you been going through a tough time, Virginie?" She virtually whispered, "Boyfriend trouble?"

"No. I'm not in a relationship. By the way, I'm a lesbian," Virginie said calmly.

An almost audible silence of disapproval rose from the jury. This was a small town with small-town values, and I had been the only juror not to swear on the bible. The judge all but rolled his eyes.

Olivia managed an incredible double take and appeared to choke with sudden confusion. She simpered, "Oh, I see. Oh, OK, forgive my ignorance," in staged surprise. She had been rehearsing this all morning in the bathroom mirror and was delighted with how well she had delivered it.

I hung my head. Virginie was doomed.

PEOPLE PERSON

Chapter Six

"I'm back with the food, Mum," Virginie called. She had begun to organize the household from the age of nine. Occasionally, it was easier to skip school and get the cleaning, the shopping, and the cooking done for the week. By now, as a young teenager, she was a competent housekeeper—frugal and industrious.

She made endless lists and then carried out her own instructions exactly as written. No one else read them, so her appalling spelling never improved. Today, her shopping list read:

450g red (deseray) potatos
1 leeter skimmed milk
150g sunflower seeds
2 x bags barly

Her recycled bags bulged with nutritious bargains. If the cashier at Tesco's had thought it strange that a young girl appeared to be doing a weekly food shop for a family on her own, she hadn't mentioned it.

Virginie couldn't remember exactly how this had become the status quo, but she knew she was doing the best she could for her mother, and that gave her a kind of peace. She also knew there was no question of bringing anything extra home ... anything she really fancied eating.

Virginie had hurried back from the shops with her mother's purse and a clutch of simple food in recycled plastic bags. The walk was refreshing after the grime of the house. She had raised her eyes for the first time all day and drunk in the view: horizon, birds, clouds scudding. She felt a little calm steal into her.

Hugo, who was ten now, helped her a bit with the less girly chores. He didn't mind digging in the garden or anything to do with a noisy gadget like the blender. He drew the line at dusting though. Their grandfather had never done anything to help, becoming more inert as the things he said had become more and more paranoid. Virginie liked to have him around for his gardening advice, but otherwise he did nothing except complain about the filth and confusion and wolf down the meals Virginie made. As the children got older, they noticed that he seemed red in the face and his breathing was labored. Virginie once tentatively mentioned the doctor, but he muttered something about the medical profession all being a mason conspiracy, so she left him to it.

That day, as Virginie let herself in through the sagging front door she saw that they had a visitor. A suited man was perched on the very edge of the sofa, which was covered with books and papers. He seemed not to notice the grime and was showing Virginie's mother something on a clipboard. Virginie issued a quiet greeting, which neither of them acknowledged, and she slid through to the kitchen.

Some council colleague of her mother's, she supposed. Virginie put her purchases away and began to chop an onion for the cheap lamb and barley stew she had planned for the family's dinner. She hummed happily to herself. "We'll eat at seven, Hugo?" she called to the garden.

The Medusa was impressed by the smartly-dressed man with very shiny shoes. He had carefully emerged through the corridor created by the junk and had arrived in her living room as though all respectable homes were piled high with rubbish. He had arranged his leaflets on a spare few inches of table.

He was pointing to a closely-typed list of racial groups and figures on his clipboard. "... our island is dangerously overcrowded," he continued. "An educated lady such as yourself can see the perils of unchecked immigration."

PEOPLE PERSON

Medusa nodded furiously, dislodging several curlers. At last, she was able to pinpoint the creeping sense of being hemmed in, of not having sufficient space to live in. She had always felt overcrowded. She hadn't known it was caused by foreigners.

Virginie's grandfather sat on a square inch of the sofa, looking on grimly. He didn't have time for many people but was happy to leave most of the decisions to his daughter and bicker with her about them afterwards. It was easier than having to deal with anyone else.

In the kitchen, Virginie didn't waste a moment. She had hung the family's coats on the back of the kitchen chairs, so while the stew was boiling she could use the hairbrush her grandfather had given her to give the coats a good brush. They were always covered with bits of fluff and dust because the house was so full of possessions. It was impossible to keep it clean. But if she could get them clean for the next time each of her family wore their coat, she would feel she had done something. Virginie knew she could just keep the dirt at bay for a short time, but if she constantly kept cleaning, dusting, and polishing, she felt she could keep the family from public humiliation and disease. It wasn't that she particularly enjoyed housework; she had just accepted it as her duty.

"Oh, Virginie! That beautiful set!"

The Medusa had evidently ventured into the kitchen to make her visitor a cup of tea.

Virginie looked guiltily at the intricate, mother-of-pearl inlay on the back of the brush in her hand. It had been a beautiful dressing table set with its matching, long-handled mirror. But *that* she had used to construct an ice-skating scene in a shoe box with Hugo. After all, what was the point of a possession, however beautiful, if it were not put to good use?

"Sorry, Mummy," Virginie mumbled, abashed. "Was it tea you wanted? I'll make it–"

But it was too late. Her mother had crashed in and was displaying her usual disastrous approach to any process. She was disorganized to the point of sabotage. She started with the tea bags, then placed them on Virginie's worktop while she rummaged for cups. She had so many that ironically, they were quite hard to access. It wouldn't occur to her to put the kettle on until she had assembled milk and sugar.

Virginie couldn't get past her mother to help, so she sat down and listened to her talk. Mathilde was very taken with her visitor. "That man is a genius, Virginie. Oh, his ideas! We'll have to get him on the council. Why he was turned down before is beyond me." She waited around, chatting for some time before she thought to put the kettle on. Suddenly, the Medusa's face dropped, and she said to her daughter with horror, "Oh, I haven't bought any milk!"

Virginie looked at her mother's panicked face with real wonder. Had she genuinely no idea that Virginie was shopping weekly for the family and therefore they had had plentiful supplies for some time now? How was it possible that she didn't know this? An uneasy feeling stirred in Virginie. There were things it was becoming impossible to ignore about her mother.

Apparently, the Medusa had not noticed this at all, and she was becoming quite distressed. "Mummy, Mummy," Virginie soothed, stroking her mother's arm and trying to get her to make eye contact. "Please don't worry! We've got plenty of milk. Look!" In desperation, Virginie reached past her mother as kindly as she could. "Here it is in the fridge."

"Oh, yes. That's right." The Medusa relaxed slightly, although a slightly obsessive glint had entered her eye. Virginie's heart sank. She knew that look. What crazy suggestion was her mother about to insist on this time? "Of course, it doesn't matter if we do run out of milk because I've got all that Coffee-mate tucked away, just in case." Virginie's mother dived into a cupboard at floor level and began unpacking all the mad things she had stored in there: endless crockery and glassware, more than they could ever use, chipped and faded. She sat down on the floor and became completely absorbed in piling it all out onto the floor until she could reach the ageing packets she had squirrelled away in there.

"Yes, but Mummy, we don't need the Coffee-mate, do we? We've got the real milk, haven't we ...?" Virginie tried to make herself heard over the clatter of pointless activity, but it was no use. In the end, Virginie finished making the tea and left her mother to happily rearrange her possessions while she took the cups out to the man in the living room.

PEOPLE PERSON

Chapter Seven

The sun had moved around and was now piercing through the blinds, leaving bars of golden light across the table and the plastic package we all considered. From my side of the table, the neat pencil letters on the package read:
90/80/13 repraH edlihtaM
Virginie's birthday. I tried not to think about that.
Our lunch arrived on a silver foil tray: curly sandwiches and limp salad. The bailiff reminded us that we were not to communicate with the outside world until we had reached our decision. He had already taken our mobile phones away in a cloth bag.
As he ate, Jake was expounding his theory about who had swung the fateful table leg. He had seized on the evidence of Virginie's brother, Hugo.
"He was a big lad, almost as big as me! He wanted to protect his smaller sister, be a man and do the right thing by his family. What did he say–?" Jake broke off to grab at the testimonies we had been given and flicked through to find Hugo's. Irene helped him locate the right one in the pile.
"But he wasn't there all day when it happened," said the 'pierced lip' juror I found out was called Annie. "The police told us that."

"Aha!" Jake roared, ignoring the interruption. "He said, *'I loved them both to bits, but there was a hell of an atmosphere in that house. I moved to Manchester to get away from them both. You could tell something was going to happen.'*"

There was an older man on the jury who had taken a shine to Irene. They were at one end of the long table, and she was quietly telling him about her divorce. He was shaking his head and occasionally said, "Good heavens," when she revealed some unchivalrous behaviour by her ex-husband.

Watching the two of them, I remembered the way Virginie would confide in her grandfather. He had been a strange, withdrawn man, but she knew how to look after him. I could hear him saying to her, "Clear the ground, strip it right back, and start from bare earth." The two of them would stand in Virginie's garden. He would teach her, and she would work away, stooping and crouching.

"You must control nature in order to heal."

I don't know that Virginie agreed with this, but she respected her grandfather and didn't contradict him. She had told me, as a young girl she had tried his approach to gardening, and they had both been delighted with the results. She was a natural. Everything she touched seemed to thrive.

Jake was clearly irked to have lost his audience. He tried to interrupt Irene and the old man's murmured conversation. "What do you say, sir?" he asked across the table. "Young man saves his sister's life?"

It was clear that Irene and the old man were far more interested in one another than in the debate around the table. The old boy said to Jake in a throw-away tone, "It is possible that the young lady saved her own life. Or perhaps, she was acting in the greater good," before Irene continued with her murmured account of her failed marriage and the two of them were engrossed once more.

No. This was far too close to the truth for me to let it pass. I quickly reminded Jay that he had decided that the murder weapon was too heavy for Virginie to have lifted, then he reiterated the point, and the other jurors chimed in to agree with him. They moved on to discussing various other male suspects, and I breathed again. Thank God.

I hadn't wanted to steer my fellow jurors so directly, but that had been something of an emergency. What I needed to do was stick to

PEOPLE PERSON

Virginie's plan of gentle, rational persuasion. She had also recommended that I get to know the jurors to influence them. I needed to work on that, and fast.

This was typical of Virginie's approach to life, and I loved her for it. Her grandfather would say, "The gardener must master the plant," but Virginie told me that she had soon realized that her success lay in working *with* the plants. The more she got to know them, the more they flourished. And while her grandfather instructed her in how to extract concentrated medicinal substances from the plants, she preferred to make diluted, holistic versions. For example: he would show her how to simmer the water from peppermint stalks to make an intoxicating oil, which was highly antiseptic, but Virginie preferred to make a cooling jelly of the leaves, which was gently effective but did not burn the skin.

I wished I had her soothing, peppermint temple balm with me to ease the tension of having to manipulate eleven people and ensure the correct verdict was reached. But I had removed every trace of her from my life, so no one would connect the two of us. I searched my bag for some alternative and found paracetamol tablets. I swallowed two with a slight shudder, knowing that the effect would be more extreme and yet infinitely less comforting.

ALEX SPEAR

PEOPLE PERSON

Chapter Eight

Virginie stepped carefully through the corridor between the clutter, her eyes never leaving the brimming tea cups she held in each hand. She managed to give one to the suited man with the very shiny shoes who perched on the edge of the sofa, the seat being covered with books, broken toys, clothes, and more books.

Virginie's grandfather was sitting next to him on the sofa, and the two of them were uncomfortably close, there being so little space to choose from. Virginie's hand shook slightly as she handed her grandfather his tea, and he said with some alarm, "Mind the books," and began to mop obsessively at them with a handkerchief though not a drop had spilled.

As she stood precariously in a tiny space between waist-high piles of stacked newspapers, Virginie strained her eyes to read the printed sheet on the visitor's clipboard resting on his lap. She could make out the words 'Restoring Local Pride.'

"Teachers would get the respect they deserve," the man was saying, "as pillars of the community; authority figures again. Children would learn British history, war studies, the kings of England, and would attend Christian assemblies. Schools would once again become institutions of order and discipline."

Virginie was confused by this. She loved school as it was and already considered it a wonderful haven of order. "What about Femi?" she blurted out.

The two men turned to the tiny girl as if seeing her for the first time.

"What's that?" asked her grandfather, beginning to mop again.

"Femi ... she, er ..." Virginie almost lost her nerve in the face of the tall stranger, who was now smiling indulgently down at her. "She's a girl in my class. She's not a Christian. She won't like an assembly about Jesus and things. She believes in, erm ..." Virginie racked her brains for the right words. "Allah, I think, or Mecca."

"Oh, no, no, no," chided the man. "No Muslim assemblies, my dear. Not in this country." He drew himself up to his full height. "Not while I have my strength."

The Medusa eventually emerged from the kitchen, evidently satisfied that they had sufficient Coffee-mate. She engaged the man in noisy conversation, standing in the middle of the piles as there was nowhere to sit down.

"It's these foreign immigrants that have caused the drug crime round here," the man was explaining to Virginie's grandfather. The suited stranger sounded very sure he was right. "And it's these homosexuals and lesbians that are causing the breakdown of the family unit and society in general, subjecting children to their pretend marriages. Decent people like ourselves need to take action before it's too late."

Virginie found it very strange that her mother seemed to want the man to like her. Normally, the Medusa seemed the strongest, most confident person Virginie knew, and other people had to try and make *her* like *them*. Medusa was slightly flushed and looked much younger than usual. She outlined her plan to get him a seat on the local council, and the visitor looked smugly pleased by this. Virginie slipped away to the kitchen, troubled.

Most of what had been said was beyond Virginie. She knew some of the words, like 'drug crime' and 'lesbian,' but she couldn't really understand the grown-up conversation and soon forgot what she had heard. But what had that man been trying to say about school and teachers?

School was Virginie's haven, a place with certainty, and the thought of any changes there made her feel sick.

PEOPLE PERSON

She thought of Miss Long, who was an authority figure if anyone was. She remembered her kind face when she had sat Virginie down at playtime and asked her if everything was all right at home. Virginie's heart had threatened to explode from her chest in response to the question. What was Miss Long implying? That she, Virginie, was not working hard enough to ensure that everything *was* all right at home?

"Yes, I think so," Virginie had managed to stammer. She had mentally run through her shopping list for the week. "I think we've got enough food and everything." She had pointed her toes behind her, under her chair, to try to conceal the horrible shoes she had been wearing due to another loss within the house. No socks that day either.

The teacher had smiled. "That's good. Your mother is certainly a busy lady, isn't she? I went to a public meeting at the Town Hall last night, and I heard her speak. I do admire her."

Virginie had agreed wholeheartedly. Despite it all, she did love her mother. And when they were not suffocating one another, she could admire her might and passion. "I try to help her as much as I can," Virginie had said. This understatement had given Miss Long a false sense that all was well in the Harper house, and there had been no further welfare checks.

Peering round the kitchen door at her mother's visitor, Virginie now felt an uneasy sense that, for the first time she could remember, her mother was not in control. This suited man seemed to assume he knew best, and the Medusa was unnaturally obedient with him. Virginie felt a shift in the balance of power within the Harper house that left it even more precarious than before.

ALEX SPEAR

PEOPLE PERSON

Chapter Nine

Rita was dying for a cigarette, so we called for the bailiff to escort us all downstairs. The jury had to remain together, quarantined from the rest of the world. We trooped down from our deliberation room to the area where we had watched the jurors' video, waiting while the front car park was cleared of bystanders.

The bailiff returned and confirmed we could go outside. As we filed past the reception desk, I made sure I did not make eye contact with the voluptuous woman in the peacock green, satin turban who sat behind the desk. She also ignored me, as if we had never met.

Rita seemed to have lit up and smoked half her first fag before we'd even arrived in the court's car park. I took my opportunity to stand next to her and make small talk. "Could I possibly have one of those?" I asked.

"Yes, my love. Are you a smoker?" she asked.

"I've given it up, but every now and then, you know ...."

"Oh, you're lucky," she puffed, holding out the gold packet to me, hardly stopping her violent inhalations, sucking the cigarette and causing the embers to crackle. "I can't do that. It's all or nothing for me."

The others were huddled farther away. It was a very cold day, and they had found a vent to crowd around that was emitting warm air. I pulled on my cigarette and lowered my voice. "I hope you don't my asking, but what was your son accused of?"

She gave me a frosty look.

"Er, you mentioned ... the last time you were here? You said he got six months?"

"It was the helicopters," Rita said with vigor.

"Helicopters?" I asked, sounding more incredulous than I'd meant to. What did he do, steal them?

"The government lied to us," Rita said firmly. "They issued a news statement that said there was no helicopter shortage. But Lee wrote to me every week, and he said they never had enough helicopters. Everyone in Basra knew it."

She lit her next cigarette from the half cigarette she was smoking. She efficiently sucked in about a litre of smoke and held it in her lungs while she said, "Well, Reginald Pathaway," then blew it out impressively.

I waited while she dragged again.

She continued, "He said he'd increase military spending, so they'd have plenty of helicopters. He told me to my face."

"Sorry, I don't know much about the armed forces. Was a lack of helicopters dangerous, then?"

"Dangerous?" she spluttered and started to cough. "Dangerous?!" Her coughing sounded like a moped starting up. I wondered if she would be able to finish her thought. She didn't so much inhale, she rattled. "It was suicide," she finally managed.

Some of the other jurors were looking over curiously. Blocking their view, I sat Rita down on the low wall.

"Suicide," she explained, shaking her head. "They had to move the men on foot, you see, through the towns and the desert. They kept being shot at by the ..." she struggled to recall the right word, "*insurgents*. And they had to walk across areas filled with landmines. Lee's best mate, Terence, lost both his legs that way." She sucked in smoke and held it while she said, "It damaged my poor Lee's head. Post-traumatic stress." Then whoosh, she blew out her smoke.

This could be an 'in.' "Soldiers ... they're not like other people, are they?" I began.

She narrowed her eyes at me. "What d'you mean?"

I rambled on as if each thought was just occurring to me, "I mean, they have to be so brave, don't they? Putting their lives in danger and

PEOPLE PERSON

defending themselves." I pulled on the cigarette to avoid her suspicious gaze. "I mean ... How many of us have actually had to kill or be killed?"

She was the one to look away now. Her eyes dropped to the ground.

"How many of us have actually taken a life," I said more quietly. "It's the hardest thing to ask a person to do, isn't it? Even though they know it's the right thing to do ... for the greater good ... it still goes against–"

"Yes, I'm very proud of my Lee," Rita interrupted, stubbing out her half-smoked cigarette with finality. "He's a hero."

I realized I would have to move fast. She seemed about to stalk back to join the rest of the group. "So, was that it then? Was that why he got a six-month jail sentence? Your Lee, he did something out there in Basra, something he was forced to because it was a 'kill or be killed' situation?"

"No," Rita said. "It wasn't out there. He was better off out there." She almost seemed about to cry, and I was shocked, even though I knew most of what she was thinking. Virginie had researched the case. "It was when he got back here. He couldn't cope with civilian life, not really, after all he'd seen. He'd been defending queen and country from these Muslims, and then he came back here, and my block was overrun with them." She was almost talking to herself now, caught up in the memory. "The girl didn't help herself. Everyone said so ... afterwards. Lee wasn't thinking straight. He's not like that. It was the stress ..." She blew her nose. "If they'd had enough *helicopters* ..." And with that she did walk away, and I had to pray I had done enough to fan the flames of a very old fire.

ALEX SPEAR

PEOPLE PERSON

Chapter Ten

Felix is a boy's name, but my mum didn't like Felice or Felicity, so there it is. I'm Felix, like the cat.

First week at uni, I met up with a few of my friends from round here. Maybe I could have done better and gone somewhere superior, but at school I had too much else on my mind to get decent marks and had fallen into a degree at Swinton, which my dad referred to as "an old Poly." It suited me. The degree was not what you'd call my priority. My priority was to meet girls.

Some of us were having lunch in the student bar and café. It was a dark, wood-paneled bar with a small strip-lit canteen area. You know the kind—cakes and quiches behind glass. I wasn't interested in the baked potatoes and baguettes. I went there for this Amaretto cheesecake they made; it was orgasmic.

The first time I saw Virginie, she was sitting alone reading a large paperback with a fierce sort of intensity. I remember noticing this girl I hadn't seen before, somehow removed from the usual student hubbub around her. Her hair had been long then, almost down to her waist, the colour of French-polished wood.

My friend, Rachel, who had been with me all through primary and secondary school, saw me looking and dug me in the ribs. "She's just your type. Go and say something!"

"Shut up, shut up," I muttered, going red. I pretended to study the beer prices on the board behind her and glanced as often as I dared at the small, quirky girl. Her shirt and jeans were charming in a hopelessly unfashionable way. "What do you mean by *my type*?"

"You know ... deep. That outfit looks like it's good for the environment or something. She's on her own. Go and speak to her now, before her mates turn up and you lose your nerve!"

I argued a bit longer, but I knew I was going to talk to her. I had to. I had never felt so intrigued by anyone before.

One of the students who worked in the canteen came out with a plate and brought it to Virginie. She smiled her thanks but carried on reading.

As I sat kicking our table leg and getting more annoyed with myself, I realized that a good ten minutes had passed, and she hadn't touched her food. She was glaring at each page of her book, making the odd note in the margin, and getting through a large section of it in a very systematic fashion.

How could she bear to wait so long to start her lunch? My general impatience was especially peaked where food was concerned. She seemed to be the opposite of me, which was fascinating. Impulsively, I stood up and went over there, ignoring Rachel's stifled shriek of encouragement.

I stood alongside Virginie's table, my hands in my pockets, horribly awkward but managing to smile at her. Thank God, the noise of all the other eaters and drinkers meant we were essentially alone. She looked up.

Enormous brown eyes.

"Er, hi. What 'ya reading?"

"Oh, er ... it's for my tutorial this afternoon." She showed me the front cover: *Horticultural Science.*

"Your lunch'll get cold," I managed, my shoulders tense and my face hot. Then I noticed that her lunch was quiche and salad.

"I'll eat it soon, when I've got my head round this topic," she said, still looking bemused but pleased I was talking to her.

I caught sight of the discreet rainbow bracelet she was wearing. I prayed this meant what I thought it meant. "Do you mind if I join–"

"Oh, please," she said, rushing to pull out a chair for me.

"I'm Felix. And yes, I know it's a boy's name."

"Virginie. I know what it's like to get comments about your name!"

PEOPLE PERSON

An awkward silence. The two of us were grinning like idiots.

"What are you studying?" she finally came up with.

"As little as I can manage, but occasionally, film."

"Film! I've hardly seen any."

"Really? You don't go to the cinema much?"

"… I have quite a lot to do at home, you see." She was shy but delighted to be talking, I could see that.

I grew bolder. "How do you get your hair to grow so beautifully long and shiny? Mine won't do that."

Her cheeks grew a little pink at the compliment, and she said, "Well, I brush it with rosemary oil." And that was how I found out about her medicinal garden.

She was fascinating. Somehow, we got on to all sorts of topics in a few minutes: from our first week at uni, to the butternut squash she couldn't get to grow, to American foreign policy, and finally, how great it was to be away from our parents. I suddenly realized how much time had passed.

"Are you going to eat your lunch?"

"Oh, yes," she said, and I noticed she wasn't smiling any more. She picked up her knife and fork as if they might explode and cut her quiche into miniscule cubes. Then she moved the salad garnish around the plate. She still hadn't eaten a bite. She dithered a bit longer, then picked up her book again. "I've forgotten one of the topics we're going to discuss. I'm just petrified the tutor will ask me a question and I'll freeze."

I couldn't stand to watch her not eat any longer. "Look, why don't I test you, and you can carry on eating?" I took the book from her.

It was the first time I had seen her hilarious writing—huge, rounded, spidery lettering littered with spelling mistakes. She was self-deprecating about it, but later, when I knew about her home life, I realized what she had lost out on. At school I'd been a lazy, class clown and got rubbish 'AS' levels. Virginie was brilliant. Get her talking and you were up against a mercurial debater, a formidable mind. If she'd had the indulged upbringing I'd had, she could have been at Oxford or Cambridge by now.

"OK. What is the collective name for the stamens?" I began.

"Androecium," she said with conviction. She speared a cube of quiche at this point and put it in her mouth. I heard her stomach growl. She put down her knife and fork to chew.

"Correct. Which part of the stamen splits to release pollen?"

"Anther," she said, calmer now. She continued to eat until half the quiche was gone, then she stopped abruptly, put her knife and fork down, and folded her hands in her lap.

"What do you call the–? Hey, Virginie, is that all you're going to eat?"

"It's a long story," she sighed. "The truth is ... I'm really not good at letting myself go." She seemed genuinely sorry.

"Really? You can't just enjoy yourself?" This concept was disturbing to me, a dedicated pleasure junkie. But I also felt a thrill. What a challenge! To make an innocent woman enjoy herself .... What could be the harm in that? "In that case, forget the quiche. I've got something you have to try. No 'buts' now, just come with me."

I led her back to the table where Rachel and the others were sitting. Rachel gave me a raised eyebrows greeting, then I sat Virginie down and introduced her to our friends. I went up to the counter to order Amaretto cheesecakes all round.

Yes, indeed,' I thought again as I glanced back to see Virginie nervously introduce herself to my noisy group of mates. What a challenge to make an innocent woman enjoy herself. It made me feel like a hero, and she deserved to let herself go. I wasn't interfering, just helping.

What could be the harm in that?

PEOPLE PERSON

Chapter Eleven

The old man was quietly telling Irene about his wife's care in hospital. "The nurses were admirable," he murmured. "Very clean ward. And they let me sit with her, long after visiting hours were over, especially in the last few weeks." His voice was as steady as ever, but Irene put a hand on his forearm.

At the next break, Irene rushed to the loo with me to put on lipstick. She was nervous and excited and said more to me than she had all morning. "I always carry it, but I forget to put it on," she gushed, looking at herself in the mirror, moving her head in nervy snaps as she scanned each angle. She was slightly flushed over her cheeks and neck.

I was glad to see that something good might come out of this trial. If they could still find it in them to love after a vicious divorce on one side and grinding bereavement on the other, then good luck to them.

I could hardly remember what life had been like before *It All Happened*, when Virginie and I had just been two kids enjoying dating. Since this chasm had opened in our lives, it took an effort to remember ever being light-hearted or carefree. I thought back to the day after I'd met her. It was a relief to mentally put my responsibility down for a few minutes' nostalgia.

I had gone downstairs to the kitchen in my shared student house. The kitchen was empty, but the TV had been yakking away like another person in the room. I wandered over to turn it off, so I could be alone. The morning light fell on the scrubbed wooden table and illuminated my breakfast.

I am very particular about giving food my full attention. Watching TV while you eat would be like undressing your lover with your eyes fixed firmly on the ceiling. I don't take my eyes off my plate until every crumb has gone.

I sat. I offered a silent prayer to the miracle that is boiled eggs and toast. I rolled the first egg to splinter the shell, then peeled away the flesh-colored pieces: squares, triangles, and hexagons. The steaming, white creature inside bounced slightly as I unwrapped it. I crusted the tip with salt, then took my first bite. Supple white yielded to crumbly golden yolk with a small, liquid center. The sudden flash of orange lit up the decapitated orb I held.

The flavour was less brash than meat, but warmer than vegetable. Iron, vitamin, and protein burst into song. In my mouth, I could feel the textures magnify—rubber, grains—as I took over a minute to savour the morsel. Looking at the gleaming white Weeble I held in my fingers, I could not bear to give up such a treasure too quickly and reached instead for a piece of toast. I looked at this little darling with lust in my eyes too. There was an expanse of brown, grainy desert quenched with inlets of pale butter, a scorch here and there to heighten the toasty pleasure.

Rachel stumped into the kitchen in her pyjamas and bunny slippers. Her hair was so big it looked as if she'd spent the night backcombing it.

"Morning," I said, crunching my toast.

"Mmmf." Rachel never has been what you'd call a morning person.

I returned to my egg. The silky nugget with flaky, orange heart felt cooler on my lips now. I placed the last of it face down on my hot, buttered toast and squashed it to make a mingled egg and butter open sandwich.

"I'm seeing Virginie again tonight," I told Rachel.

Her heavy-with-sleep face managed to grin at this. "Hey, that's great. Are you going somewhere nice?"

"She doesn't know yet, but I've got us a table at Chariot."

Chariot was the only decent restaurant in our university town that I could just about afford.

PEOPLE PERSON

"Lucky girl!"

"Yeah, I'll be broke for months, but she's worth it."

My daydream faded. Such simple, mundane conversations belonged in the past now. I wanted to cut this responsibility out of me, but I knew it powered me, and without it, I would be weak.

Returning to the table in the room where the jury must decide how much Virginie's life was worth, I paused before sitting down to choose my seat carefully. The conversation around me seemed harmless enough. The break had allowed us to briefly discuss topics other than the trial, and currently, Jay and Rita were dominating a debate about the latest war headline. I glanced round the table and noticed that Annie wasn't really interested in the conversation.

I casually strolled around the table as if stretching my legs, peering at the slits through the blinds, looking like a person trying to make out the outside world, then smiled at Annie and sat down next to her. Though she did not know it, she would be the next member of the jury to be persuaded of Virginie's innocence.

That sounds far more confident than I felt, by the way. I would fight to the death for this, but there was no guarantee that any of the plan would work.

I drew strength from my Virginie and the last words she had said to me before she had been arrested:

"All you can do is sow the seed."

ALEX SPEAR

PEOPLE PERSON

Chapter Twelve

I walked her down to the main drag where the restaurants are located. We had to jump off the pavement. So many couples were striding along hand in hand, I felt like tripping them up. Virginie couldn't risk anyone knowing we were a couple in case it got back to her mother.

"We're not going in *there*?" she said in horror as we approached Chariot.

"Why? What's wrong with it?" Through the picture window we could see the well-heeled clientele, some in business suits and some in full-on posh frocks.

"It's far too upmarket for the likes of me," Virginie almost whispered. She had put on her favourite charcoal-colored wool dress. She'd told me she'd found it in a charity shop for a few pounds. It was hard-wearing and simple. On her slight frame, it could have been Chanel. "I couldn't relax in there, Felix. Let's go somewhere ordinary, please."

"Well, OK then. You pick somewhere."

We walked on, ignoring the gilt and velvet of Chariot.

I remember that night in every detail: street lamp glow, people laughing, and the beginnings of rain.

We walked on. She seemed intimidated by most of the windows framed by stiff menus, even where the tables inside had no cloths and the patrons were sipping bottles of beer rather than glasses of wine.

I saw us reflected in one of the windows. She in her dress, which skimmed the succulent thigh area just above her kneecaps, T-bar shoes, hair piled up out of the way, a self-effacing stoop to her posture, and a skittish walk. I wore cords and a slim-fitting checked shirt. That's as dressed up as I do. My hair's cropped and bleached by the sun from surfing. I would be butch if I could be bothered.

"How about this one?" I suggested. The Olive Grove. Mid-range Greek with paper tablecloths and metal cutlery. She faltered, took a few steps towards the door, then backed away.

"Oh, I am sorry," she howled, her hands up in her hair. "What's wrong with me?"

We had reached the end of the strip and had walked almost into the darkness beyond. "There's nothing up there, only houses," I said. "Come on. Let's try again." But she held my arm.

"What's that one there?"

Through the darkness we could see a small neon sign over a house on the suburban street. As we walked nearer we saw that the sign said, 'Gaia Veg Café.'

"Is that a place you can go in?"

"Let's give it a try!" And she pulled me along.

It turned out to be a one-woman operation, the woman dishing up cheap veggie food in her converted living room. Virginie fell in love with the place.

We sat where the woman's young son showed us, at a table with benches attached, looking for all the world as if it had been stolen from a pub garden.

The woman introduced herself as Tracy and explained she'd got fed up with working for other people, so had set up her own business. Virginie was elated by this idea. When Tracy had taken our orders and disappeared into the kitchen, Virginie whispered, "I could do that!"

"What?"

"Have my own business and run it from home!"

"Not from *your* home, my love. Think of all the clutter." I didn't mean to be unsupportive, but I couldn't sensibly discuss any business idea; the thought of working voluntarily made me feel quite ill. "Don't you have to do loads of tax-y paperwork-y things?"

PEOPLE PERSON

"I don't know." She was subdued. I felt bad to have squashed her enthusiasm, so I said, "Ask her."

"Who? Tracy? Oh, I couldn't ...."

"Then, I'll ask her."

When Tracy came back with our spinach soups, I said, "Hope you don't mind me asking, but how did you go about starting up your own restaurant? My friend here is very talented," a squeak of self-deprecation came from across the table, "and we'd love to sell some of the things she makes."

"Ooh, what do you do then, my dear?" Tracy asked Virginie.

"Just alternative health and beauty type things out of herbs and plants."

"Aren't you clever! Well, it can be hard work, but it's worth it." Tracy beamed at Virginie. "My advice would be to get organized with all your records, and plan to get by without a salary for yourself for the first two years. I'll dig out a book that helped me a lot. And please feel free to drop in here for a chat if you ever get stuck."

"There you go then," I said when we were alone again. "Now, let's eat."

The soup was dark green, verging on black, and had a little spiral of cream. I had consumed half mine before I realized Virginie wasn't eating.

"What's up? Don't you like it?"

"It looks delicious," she sighed. She had been waving her spoon over the bowl, as is she were about to plunge in, then changing her mind and moving the bowl slightly, setting the spoon down, then pulling her bread roll to tiny pieces without putting a single piece in her mouth. "I've been eating in this odd way for so long, I don't know how to do it normally."

"Like this," I demonstrated. "Take a spoonful. Put it in your mouth. Swallow."

She did so. She had the spoon clutched so tightly in her fist that her knuckles were slightly white. Her spine seemed frozen in a completely upright position. Her jaw was so tense it looked an effort to open her mouth and get the spoon in. Swallowing the soup was OK though.

"Very good," I soothed. "But you're forgetting to enjoy it."

"... I can't remember how to."

"Well, try this." I thought for a moment. The enjoyment of food, sex, and life in general came naturally to me, but I have never been called upon to put it into words before. "Think about all the different flavours and textures in it. Eat slowly. No one's watching, apart from me."

She did try, but it was clearly an ordeal, even if I stopped looking at her and turned my head to look round the room. The other tables were empty. We were early and it was midweek.

By the time Tracy cleared our bowls, Virginie had managed five spoonfuls of her soup, and I had finished hers off. Next, we had a mushroom filo thing each. Virginie managed one bite of this, and then, I had to eat the rest of hers as well as mine. I was too stuffed for dessert, unheard of for me.

"I'm so sorry," she wailed as we walked home.

"Stop apologizing. I enjoy spending time with you, even if you are a freak."

She gave me a little kiss and told me not to come home with her. She ran off, and I ambled back to the campus. I missed her already.

PEOPLE PERSON

Chapter Thirteen

After our meal, Virginie had rushed home and I had not seen her at uni for days after that. I charmed the student administrator into giving me Virginie's address and went to find her.

The front door was hanging off its hinges. I gingerly pushed it open and stepped into the most horrible, squalid, little house I had ever seen, piled high with junk.

I may have lived an easy life but enough friends and fellow uni students struggled with mental health problems for me to have clue what I was seeing here. Mental wrongness can smell of booze or cigarettes or overflowing rubbish bins, but there's one thing it always smells of—sweat. Stale, grubby sweat, unwashed human skin, greasy hair, and mouldy feet. It takes a powerful, wretched chemical imbalance in the mind to make a person neglect their body like that.

There was a squawk of indignation from the center of the mess. In the gloom I discerned Virginie's mother rearing up from her nest. She sat up on her mattress on the floor. She was surrounded by boxes, curlers escaping from her head, just as Virginie had described her.

"How do you do, Mrs. Harper. Is Virginie at home? May I come in?"

"Who are you?" she demanded.

"A friend of Virginie's from university."

She shrugged and called to her daughter, "Child, there's a ... woman here to see you." She got back to rearranging the filth.

I slid through the corridor of clothes, books, and broken china tea sets to the door she had indicated. I noticed that the door handle was beautifully polished. Looking back at Virginie's mother, I got the strangest impression that the small pathway of carpet in between the heaped possessions had been recently hoovered, but the Medusa was busily making the area grubby again with her soiled possessions. What the hell was she doing? Sort of rearranging piles of ... well, *things*. Perfectly normal things, just dizzyingly bizarre in their quantities. It was as if the house was under the control of a willful child who felt if one teapot and a set of china cups was good, then twelve different teapots and fifty mismatched cups was logically even better. My hand on the door handle, I suddenly lurched and almost fell through the door as someone opened it from the inside.

I stumbled into a very much less chaotic kitchen. Virginie had just opened the internal door and she stood open-mouthed in a spotless apron.

"What are you doing here?" I could see she was embarrassed by the place. She shut the door quietly.

"I had to see you. I missed you."

The scrubbed kitchen table smelt faintly of lavender, the floor under it smelt faintly of bleach. The stacked possessions around the kitchen were encroaching on the clear central area. In my mind, confused by all the clutter everywhere, the piled items seemed to have been not so much cleared as *frightened* back slightly, so that Virginie's kitchen had the look of a clearing in a jungle. Her kettle and pots and pans stood shining and organized on the stove, the only available space apart from the table.

She made us a pot of rosemary tea. The bright infusion filled the air with a wonderful, uplifting aroma. We sat down opposite each other, and at last, she smiled. She had such a beautiful face with a frank expression and enormous, intelligent eyes.

Reaching out to stroke her face across her table, I kissed her slowly. The world went away. I felt a flutter in my belly.

"Come away from here," I begged her. "Even if it's not with me, just leave this horrible house and live your own life." I had come round with a particular plan in mind but doubted she would go for it. "Let's go away for the weekend to start with. I'll pay."

PEOPLE PERSON

"I can't. Mother could never cope. So long as I'm always there, I can just about keep the place hygienic enough to keep her safe. I don't think she'd ever clean anything. She'd pile up rubbish so high it would probably fall on her or Grandfather and no one would know."

"I know, I know, but …" I tailed off, unable to express my emotion. Back then, I didn't know how to describe what I meant. I was nineteen and had never lived a second of my life for anyone other than myself. I had never considered either of my parents as people, and the thought they might need a thing from me was laughable. I was selfish and arrogant without even knowing what an alternative might be. Virginie's world was distasteful to my immature soul. "It's not your responsibility. When are you going to be yourself, go out into the world and find out what your destiny is?"

"When the time is right," she said firmly. "Now, let's change the subject."

I didn't want to, but she jumped up and seemed about to resume her endless work, so I asked her, "Can I see your garden?"

She smiled modestly as she turned the key and threw open the door with something approaching a flourish. I just stood and stared.

Virginie's small garden was a patchwork of feathery herbs, stiff grasses, and woody bushes. There were perfectly square patches of greens, silvery-purples, and an occasional flash of orange. Surrounded by tattered fences on three sides, an area of no more than six square meters had been put to incredibly efficient use. The scent coming off the garden seemed aromatic enough to heal us from where we stood. There was something cleansing in the air.

She introduced each of her plants to me as if they were her children. Here was marigold, which could be used as an antiseptic. Garlic, onions, and leeks lowered blood pressure. In the corner were mustard seed for warming, parsley for cleansing, and chamomile for relaxation and sleep.

"How do you know all this?" I asked her, to which she replied simply, "From Grandfather," and continued our tour.

These feathery tops would be carrots, easily digested and a diuretic. A rosemary bush had been recently clipped to provide her nourishing hair oil. This patch would be barley, cooling and healing. I stepped carefully behind her as she hopped between her plants on the half bricks she had pushed into the ground to make a scattered path.

Finally, she introduced caraway for digestion and basil to clear the mind.

It was also an aphrodisiac.

Virginie gave a little smile when she said this, and I felt that flutter again.

I looked around before I surreptitiously took her hand in mine. "Listen, I wasn't just talking generally about going away for the weekend. I've seen a coach advertised in the local paper. You go to Swinton in the middle of the night, and the coach drives all the way to Amsterdam. You go in the small hours of Saturday morning and you're back home by the Sunday evening."

"*Amsterdam?*" she whispered, incredulous. "I've never been anywhere. But what would we do?"

"We could hang out in coffee shops and have a go at smoking dope properly. You've not tried it before, have you? There's loads of stupid art galleries and stuff that you'll love, and bars to have a beer in ... but think about it ..." I grinned, my voice low, "we can stay in a hotel room. Just the two of us. For a whole night."

She got her saucy look. My fluttering stomach threatened to become airborne.

We hadn't slept together. My shared room in halls made sex possible but not exactly luxurious, and with Virginie, I wanted it to be special. It was not a turn-on for either of us that my roommate could return at any moment.

"Well, I'd love to go," she said, finally, but I really haven't got a penny."

"Don't you worry about that, little lady," I puffed. I'd worked out I could just barely scrape the money together for both our tickets on the thankfully cheap coach. "You leave everything to me."

PEOPLE PERSON

Chapter Fourteen

I knocked quietly on her front door. It was still as dark as it had been all night. She came out straight away, with a tiny holdall and the hood of her coat up. Her face was small and white.

"All right?" I whispered, grinning.

"Well, I s'pose, but Mother was so upset when I told her ...."

"Now, look. We've been over this. You'll be away for less than forty-eight hours. She's not a *child*." I grabbed her holdall and slung it over my own rucksack. I turned and started walking at a brisk pace. "We'll need to go some if we don't want to miss the coach. They don't wait." I didn't turn my head, afraid she might not be there, but after a minute, I realized she was following and I slowed slightly. She caught up with me, hopping along like a little bird. I took her hand. She was freezing.

As we walked along in silence, her anxiety seemed to fill the air like a terrible heartbeat. I could almost hear her internal monologue. *What if Mother wakes up in the night and feels frightened? She often wakes me for reassurance, but tonight, I won't be there. What if Hugo comes home late and drunk and starts an argument? What if Grandfather thinks it's the war again and goes to hide on the common like last time and dies of the cold?*

But I pulled her on, relentlessly. If she didn't make this tiny bid for freedom, what else of her life would she sacrifice?

We made the coach in time, and I slept most of the way to Centraal Station. Virginie held my hand the whole way and stared out the window at the black motorway.

Around four, I woke briefly and pulled her to me for a hug, concealed by the high seat backs. "What are you thinking about?" I asked her sleepily.

"Just being away, you know. I've hardly got any *stuff* with me. I couldn't decide what to bring, so I hardly brought anything."

"Does it feel weird?"

"*Really* weird ... but good. I feel free."

We fell off the coach at our destination. The sun was coming up. The sight of the stunning façade of Centraal and the noise of a cluster of crazy accordion players in the entrance woke us up. Virginie and I just looked at each other and she screamed, "Oh! We're in Amsterdam!" She jumped up and down and hugged me.

It was like being in a shared dream. We pulled our bags over our shoulders and walked along the canals to the hotel I'd booked.

She pointed out everything, talking and laughing and wondering and enjoying. She loved the architecture, all gothic stonework and details picked out in gold. It was peaceful and shady under the trees as we walked along in the fresh morning, and people from the cafés were unstacking chairs and bringing out signboards. We didn't notice our aching muscles from sitting in the cramped coach seats across Europe. I'd spent as little as I could on the transport because I needed the money for a private hotel room; I didn't want us in a youth hostel, in bunk beds, or sharing a room with anyone else.

We reached the hotel with the help of a tiny, creased map given to us by a young waiter from one of the cafés. I dealt with the booking, and we climbed up a treacherous spiral staircase to reach our room.

My hand was strangely sweaty and useless as I tried to fit our key in the lock. After fumbling for a minute, I swore, and Virginie took over. She managed to get the door open, and we burst into the room.

Our room was small and bare, with low twin beds and rough, handwoven covers: one pink, one blue. There was a tiny bathroom ensuite. Huge windows let in the Amsterdam morning light.

We each sat on a bed. I let our bags drop to the floor.

"Are you, ah ... Are you OK with that bed?" I asked.

PEOPLE PERSON

"Yes."

"Shall we, ah ..."

"Push them together? Oh, yes!" She jumped up to do it. I pushed my bed to meet hers, then we both crawled to the middle and knelt on the hard, middle section. I held her slight, muscular body to me. She looked at me for a moment, then kissed me.

Virginie has got the most incredible mouth. It's slightly over-sized, with pouting lips top and bottom. Kissing her always seems to taste of something delicious and wholesome. The closest I can come to describing it is to say it's like spiced gingerbread. I let my hand creep under her shirt at the back and felt the delicate structure of her back. She ran a hand over my cheek, my jaw.

Being so close to her made me feel a little dizzy and intoxicated.

I put my head on her shoulder and slowed my breathing. "Shall we ... Shall we go and explore, er, first, you know ...?"

"Yes," she breathed. "But let's not be too long."

PEOPLE PERSON

Chapter Fifteen

We went in to our first coffee shop. Its name was carved in wood outside. It was on various floors and had a tiny spiral staircase, which seemed to be a feature of Amsterdam. There were low, wooden stools before tables and the sofas were upholstered in geometric shapes. We sat down and looked at each other nervously.

"What do we do?" Virginie hissed.

"How should I know?"

A gorgeous blonde waitress strolled by. "Ladies?" she enquired. Though she had a Dutch accent, her English was perfect. "You want some drinks?"

"Er …" I lost it.

"Please could I have a cup of tea? And my friend will have a beer," Virginie piped up.

When we were alone again, I muttered, "What about the dope? It's legal here, right? So, do you just come out and say it, or do they keep it in a back room, or what …?"

"What's everyone else doing?" Virginie whispered, looking furtively around.

We saw the odd Dutch person turn up, smoke a joint from somewhere behind the bar, then saunter off looking chilled. Our drinks arrived. Virginie's tea was black, meaning a subtle blond in color, clearly visible through the clear, glass cup. I glugged my frosty beer. Presently, we ordered expensive croissants with apricot jam, which Virginie tore to pieces but couldn't seem to put in her mouth. I was just dabbing up the last crumbs of mine when our waitress appeared and said nonchalantly, "You wanna spliff now?"

We both erupted in the affirmative at once. How cool.

We ended up buying a bag of grass called Northern Lights. I made a joint and showed Virginie how to share it without getting the end all damp. I showed her how to hold the smoke in her lungs without coughing. The Northern Lights was very strong, and before the whole joint was gone, we were both collapsed in giggles.

I made another, then another. Hours slipped by. We kept trying to leave for the art gallery but could not manage it. Virginie's beautiful face was more open than I'd ever seen it. The tiny lines of tension in her forehead were gone.

She leant back against the wall behind her seat and drawled, "I ... feel ... so ... *relaxed* ...."

"You look wonderful. Beautiful."

"... and ... I'm hungry!" She picked up a piece of her croissant and ate it with more relish than I've ever seen with her.

"Can I ask you about your eating, Virginie?" I began tentatively. I'd wanted to find out what was going on there since we met, but we still didn't know each other all that well. We'd only been together a couple of months, but cannabis brings down your barriers, doesn't it?

She gave a big sigh. "It's hard to explain," she said, then devoured more croissant. "I *can* eat. It's not like I'm anorexic or anything. It's just ... I always feel so ... kind of ... stressed, and, um ..." She furrowed her brow to think of the word, then shook her head as she gave up. "I just always feel kind of ... like I have to be completely in control all the time, to keep the house running, and keep Mummy and Grandfather safe. It's like I have to be disciplined, but I'm ... surrounded by all this chaos ... and so, I ... so, I ..." She tailed off and stared over my head.

I followed her gaze. She was eyeing the daily specials written up there.

"I think I get what you mean," I said. She looked at me with some surprise. "You've said before, you can never really let go."

"That's right!" she grinned with a real stoner expression. It was adorable on her. "I can never ... really ... let go ... and eating is kind

PEOPLE PERSON

of ... like ... this thing I can really ... concentrate on ... and do it perfectly ... like cut the food up really precisely ... and be really ... *restrained* ... about ... how much I eat. Most people eat far too much ... far, far too much ...."

"You want to eat something now?" I was making another fat joint. I love my food, and right then, I had the munchies.

"Ooh, yes ... I've never felt so hungry ...."

We slowly ate our way through enormous fried breakfasts, then pot brownies and elaborate hot chocolates. I finally saw Virginie eat the way you're supposed to eat—with sensuality, transported by pleasure. We slipped into private meditation, occasionally coming to and laughing to each other.

"Enjoying yourself?"

"Oh, yes!"

I squeezed her leg under the table. "Smoking dope suits you, baby. We should do this when we're back home."

"But it's illegal?"

"No one cares if you have a little. You could grow it in your garden. You can grow anything."

She looked torn. "It would be lovely to feel like this now and then ... but how?"

"You can buy the seeds here."

Our waitress appeared to clear the plates. She had brought us a little bag of shriveled brown buds. "Try this sinsemilla," she said. "It's especially for you: female buds grown in the absence of male plants." She gave me a lewd wink.

When we were alone again, I said, "The seeds are tiny."

"Wouldn't they find them at customs? We might get searched."

"And they have sniffer dogs."

"Do the seeds smell?" she whispered.

"I think they do, a bit. Could we hide them in something with a strong smell?"

A voice behind us said, "Just post them."

We both jumped out of our skins. Our waitress was standing nearby listening in. We were both too stoned to have noticed her there.

"Post?"

"Yeah, loads of tourists do it, and they tell me it works. Send the seeds to yourself and you probably won't get caught. If they do, er, er ..." she tried to remember the English word, "*detect* it, they'll destroy it

- 63 -

and send you a card to say someone's trying to send you illegal stuff through the post. You claim you've got no idea about it; just a person sending it for a big joke."

"Ha, ha. Yes, we were only joking," I said. "We're not really going to do anything illegal …."

"Spliff should be legal everywhere," our waitress said with passion. "Here in Holland, we understand if you treat people like adults they are responsible."

"I agree!" Virginie chimed in. "It's amazing what people can do if they have to live up to a challenge."

"What about us adults who want to live like children?" I drawled, making both women giggle pleasingly.

We gave up the art gallery and staggered back to the hotel. The spiral staircase was insane, and we took each other's hand and swayed up slowly.

Virginie threw herself down on her side of the bed. She gave me a wonderful, stoned, sexy look.

That moment, in that room together, was not a time for holding back. We had fought for this freedom, and restraint would have been a crime.

PEOPLE PERSON

Chapter Sixteen

I had to shake myself out of my recollection and bring my mind back to the unfolding trial.

Annie was one of those tiny women I can hardly believe are real. She looked incredibly petite in the chair at the polished table, and I had to slouch to make proper eye contact. She must have been less than five feet tall. She was so slender and delicate that she looked like a perfect, little doll. Or rather, she would have done without the severe, black hair with an inch of brown roots, the piercings, and the black lipstick. She wore spider web earrings.

The conversation going on at the other end of the table provided a diversion for the other jurors. I quietly brought Annie back to the case we were considering. "Any idea how you'll find? I mean, what do you think of this, er ... Virginie?"

"I just don't get how she stayed in that situation for so long," she began with a shudder. "I mean, you've got to live your own life, haven't you? That's what we're all here for, isn't it?"

"You're sure she did do it then?" I asked her.

"Oh, yes," said Annie with conviction. "It's the only explanation that makes sense psychologically, don't you think? No one else had such an intense relationship with the dead woman—not her father, not her son. Her and her daughter were locked in battle every day, it seems. Who else would *care* enough to kill her?"

A chill stole into me. I wondered if she could possibly know the truth. But if she did, why was she telling me?

"I've had one like that," Annie continued, snapping me back to reality.

"One what?"

"Relationship. That intense. You feel you'll either kill or be killed. It's volatile, and you know something really destructive is going to happen."

I glanced around to check that no one else was listening in. No, we were still OK, not overheard.

I was losing my grip on the story. Towards the end, Annie seemed to be describing not Virginie and her mother, but Virginie and me. But she couldn't know about that. Like an under-prepared actor on a merciless stage, I was in danger of fluffing my lines here.

I decided to steer the conversation to her own life. "Who was he, then?"

She smiled. "One of his names was ... Ion." She said it in hushed tones, whether in honour or fear, I couldn't tell. "A Romany name."

"Were you together long?"

"A few months, but it felt like a lifetime. And I'm sure he saw other girls at the same time as me. But it didn't matter somehow. When he was with me it was so intense. Nothing else mattered, you know?"

Careful, don't let the mask slip. "Yeah, I guess." A sudden hunch occurred to me, and I decided to act on it, though it was a terrible risk. "Annie ... this Ion ... was he ever violent?"

"No. He never raised a hand to me," she said firmly. "But to a man who deserved it ..." She tailed off, and I knew I had been right.

"Did he ever kill anyone?" She couldn't meet my eye now. "I'm sorry, I didn't mean to pry. It's just ... I was wondering whether you had first-hand knowledge of this kind of case? It makes your decision more important somehow, if you really know what makes a person kill."

Her face told me she was thinking about Virginie in a new light now: as a passionate human being, no less entitled to kill than the impressive Ion. Of course, this was why Virginie had chosen Annie for the jury. She was in a similar position to me, though she didn't know it.

PEOPLE PERSON

I turned away and left her to her thoughts.

PEOPLE PERSON

Chapter Seventeen

This is how Virginie and I made love for the first time.

She was lying back, one hand over her heart. I pulled her arm away. I put my hand gently on her breast and moved in close, so I could kiss her mouth.

She tugged at my top as she kissed me back deeply, exploring my mouth with her tongue.

Quite suddenly, she sat me up and helped me ease my top off over my head. She threw it on the floor. My skin incredibly sensitive under her touch, I breathed as she ran her fingertips from the waistband of my jeans, over my belly, up as far as my bra, and back down again.

I unbuttoned her shirt. She had a T-shirt under it and a body top under that. We laughed as I struggled.

"You're like ... a thing with lots of layers," I muttered.

"An onion ... an artichoke ...."

With her many tops finally off, I caught a wonderful lemony scent from her warm skin. I kissed her neck, then her shoulder, then pecked kisses over her breasts.

She rolled us both over, and we fought our jeans off. She was surprisingly strong. She seemed delighted and took her time looking at me, running her hands all over.

I could hardly believe we were here. I had fantasized about it so many times. She moved with me, my leg between her thighs. She made me feel crazy. I was shaking, or maybe she was. Trying to be gentle, I slid my hand under the cotton of her knickers. Her beautiful sex felt slippery and neat. She stuffed her fist in her mouth when I touched her.

I wanted her to touch me at the same time. I took her hand and guided it down. I showed her how to use her fingertips and where. The two of us worked each other, shuddering and panting.

Nerves made things slow, and we were in danger of arm cramps, so I gathered her to me and used my middle finger to drive into her. She yelped as I entered her. In a sweet moment, she was rigid with a gasp, waves of pleasure moving through her slender, strong body.

When she was still, I finished myself off, clinging to her. We were soaked in sweat, and her long hair was stuck to my temples. She put her forehead against mine, and we seemed to commune in silence. Then we started again.

There was no stopping her now. She rolled me over and stroked my back and bottom till I was desperate for her again. I turned, and she seized me, and we slid over each other, up and down, up and down, running with sweat, beyond speech.

Virginie held me down and fucked me. I don't think I've ever felt so *used* in such a good way. I burst into tears and begged her not to stop. Her hand was inside me, seeming to pull at the core of me. She gazed into my eyes as we communicated in this ancient way. We were clumsy and fumbling as we tried our best, both inexperienced and both so desperate to make the other feel good. I felt myself come more than once under her passionate attentions. Sobbing and gulping for air, I finally grabbed her hand and she was instantly still. I grimaced as she eased out of me.

Calming my breath, I kissed her, then shuffled her round on her back and placed my mouth between her legs. She writhed under me as I explored my favourite part of her. My tongue found salty folds and a hot, open channel. She slowly relaxed as she got used to the sensation. I tried to remember how I had felt the first time someone had gone down on me, and I made my tongue wide and soft and gentle. I could have got the sugar off a cappuccino without disturbing the froth. As she grew closer, I pressed a little harder, my tongue more of a dart. She

PEOPLE PERSON

groaned, and I gave her a barrage of feathery, side-to-side strokes until suddenly, her hips moved, and I was all but bucked off.

I longed to take her again, make her feel all the pleasure she had denied herself, but we were both exhausted. I held her and was overjoyed to see her expression: satisfaction without self-reproach.

Each of us wordlessly vowed, in our lovers' eye contact, never to live with compromise again. Restraint was for others who had not found love like this.

ALEX SPEAR

PEOPLE PERSON

Chapter Eighteen

We held hands the whole way home to Swinton. I couldn't stop grinning at her.

Sealed by sex, our love now seemed indestructible. We felt as invincible as only young people can. Everything had changed. Her mother, her mad house and home life—they were nothing now; all gone.

In our private world on the coach home, screened by high seat backs, we shared a picnic for lunch. Virginie opened a small pot of olives we had bought. She picked one up between thumb and forefinger and held it up to my lips. I opened my mouth, and she pushed the olive in. As the flavours burst in my mouth, I could taste the chunks of preserved lemon the olives had been steeped in. My senses sharpened by the intense, salty fullness in my mouth, I picked up a half-moon of tomato, glossy with olive oil, and fed it to Virginie. She devoured it with a shy smile of sensuality. Then she pulled me to her and kissed me. Salt, oil, oregano, and that maddening undercurrent of spiced gingerbread.

We arrived back at the bus stop in Swinton at dusk. We had agreed that we would not tell her family about us. Virginie believed the shock could unhinge them completely. It was enough that we knew, that we could each cuddle up to the private thought of our love. Virginie seemed to dance home.

I walked her to her front gate and was about to leave her when we noticed the demolished front wall. Bricks had exploded in a half moon and were covering the crazy garden. Virginie's mother's car was parked in its usual spot on the road nearby, but the bonnet was slightly crumpled and very scratched.

Virginie could not get the front door to the house open at first and was beside herself with anxiety when she could get no reply to her frantic ringing of the doorbell. That battered front door that normally hung off its hinges was now firmly wedged against the frame and would not budge. I shoved against the door with her, and we managed to get it to move. The base of it seemed to have warped in the rain.

Virginie's mother was sprawled on the floor. Virginie ran to her and knelt. The Medusa was very pale and looked frail. Through Virginie's staccato questioning, it became clear that her mother had neglected to eat or drink anything since Virginie had departed, some thirty-six hours earlier. It also emerged that Virginie's grandfather had run amok, driving the family car into the front wall and fleeing to the common where he had hidden during the war.

Virginie cradled her mother's head and gently helped her to sip from a glass of water. I ran to the common, swearing. It was starting to rain.

I found the old coot huddled under a bush. "Come on, Victor," I barked at him. He stared at me without seeing. I half pulled, half frog-marched him back to their horrible house. He managed to get away at one point, running into the road with an ensuing honking of horns and a squealing of brakes. I grabbed his skinny shoulders and hauled him back to the safety of the pavement. He was calmer after that and meekly walked home with me.

When we arrived back, Mr. Patel from up the road was helping clear the bricks with his son. They had brought a wheelbarrow round with them. Virginie's brother was nowhere to be seen.

Inside, I could smell that Virginie was burning turmeric and cinnamon on her stove to cleanse her kitchen. I opened the internal door attempting to perfume the rest of the sweaty, stale house.

Virginie sat her grandfather down in his favourite spot in the living room, in the middle of his maze of books, and he started to add to it. He tenderly placed each one on his wall as expertly as a bricklayer,

PEOPLE PERSON

happily sitting amidst them, suddenly calmed. Virginie disappeared into the kitchen and quickly reappeared with a meal for us all. She attempted to hand a plate of steaming poached eggs on toast to her grandfather, but he indicated that she was to wait until he had created the latest section of his barrier. Her mother devoured her dinner, sitting on a pile of newspapers.

I suppose it was that night that I realized Virginie would never be mine, so long as her mother and grandfather were alive.

ALEX SPEAR

PEOPLE PERSON

Chapter Nineteen

A few days later, Rachel had told me that some of the students in our year had arranged to take a year out, mid-degree, and travel round Australia together. She wondered if Virginie and I would like to come.

Immediately, I said to count me in. Abandoning the distasteful hard work of my degree for months of sunbathing and surfing was just my style. I suppose we both knew that Virginie would never leave her mother. Rachel was probably just inviting her to be polite, but hearing her say it, gave me some crazy hope. We were to leave in early September, shortly after Virginie's twenty-first birthday. It felt like a rite of passage I had to force her to take.

I was waiting for her in her kitchen, trying not to overhear the conversation she was having with her mother in the horrible living room. It was a conversation I had heard before.

"Mother, this is open."

I could picture Virginie holding the envelope, drawn up to her full five-foot-one frame.

"Yes. Yes, child. I couldn't see the name without my glasses."

I could imagine her mother, at once overbearing and weak, maddening in her transparent deceit.

Virginie was audibly trying to keep her voice steady. "You said that the last time, Mother. And the time before that, you said you mistook 'Miss' Harper for 'Mrs.'."

As with other similar arguments I had overheard, I was sure the confused old woman's eyes would be darting around, trying to remember what had happened. Her eyes would probably fall back onto a tiny spot on the sofa, barely able to keep a grip on what was going on right now. As ever, Virginie would become infuriated, provoked by her exhaustion from the endless cleaning and caring for her mother, and she would accidentally raise her voice. "You can't open my post. It's private. It's none of your business. You must understand that, surely?"

"What secrets can you have from your mother?"

That was a new one. What was the old hag up to now?

There was silence for a moment, and I strained my ears to hear Virginie's reaction.

"What do you mean?" she asked, and her voice was no longer so strong.

"A boyfriend? Who is he?" the Medusa suddenly demanded. "Some snake, taking you away from your family where you're needed!"

"I don't have a boyfriend, Mummy."

I could not hear her mother's muttered response. After a pause, the kitchen door opened and Virginie stepped slowly into the room.

She looked very thin.

"Sorry about that," Virginie said and shook her head as if to clear it. She closed the door, listened for a moment, then came over to give me a furtive kiss. She stood in front of me, one hand over her mouth, bashful yet delighted.

"Any sign of our envelope?" I hissed. The cannabis seeds still hadn't turned up.

"Don't think so," she whispered back. "Mummy always makes a huge fuss when I get anything through the post. She seems to hate it. I doubt whether she would have just thrown it away." She breathed and smiled. "Now then, where are we off to?"

I was grinning from the kiss. I couldn't help it. "I thought the cinema. There's a film I could do with seeing for my course—might make up for not doing any work all year."

"Or we could just go back to your place," she breathed, kissing me again.

PEOPLE PERSON

We were both flushed red with her boldness. She was rarely so direct, and it was thrilling.

"OK," I stammered back.

"I've just got a few things to do first," she said, all serious again. She put on a gleaming white apron and tied it behind her.

Virginie had begun to package some of her herbal products for sale. She found it more economical to make large quantities and therefore had a surplus over what her little household could use.

Today, she had made a lavender salve. She melted it on the stove in a battered little pan, then poured it into old, sparkling clean jam jars.

The thought of my horrible room in halls wasn't appealing. I wanted somewhere beautiful to be with her ... like a beach in Australia. "Come away with me again," I blurted out.

She looked at me in surprise. I had meant to lead up to it. I levelled with her and told her all about going round Australia. She just had to come with me.

I tried to wear her down. I thought I had an answer to every objection. We would take out bank loans and spend the first five years of our working lives paying them back. When else can you do such mad, wonderful things if not in your early twenties? The crowd I was going with were scornful of the weights that held our parents down: marriages, children, and property. When else would we have the energy and the optimism to just take off?

But Virginie wouldn't. She couldn't. Unlike the rest of us, she already had caring responsibilities. Like a child she hadn't chosen to give birth to, her mother needed her to stay close in monotonous, daily drudgery.

So, with the selfishness only possible at that age, I chose to go without her. If she was hurt, she didn't let it show.

She carried on with her busy-ness and her productivity. A swirl of natural purple coloring made the rich lavender butter look particularly beautiful. She had boiled grape skins to achieve this. Screwing the lids back on, she added pretty gingham cloth covers and labels written in her spidery handwriting with the terrible spelling.

The pots looked good enough for any alternative beauty product shop, but we didn't know anyone in business who could help us, so Virginie just sold them out of a box in her front garden. She was a born saleswoman, her mercurial conversation bringing customers back again and again. She was shrewd and made a modest profit from her hard work. She kept the money secretly in what she called her 'one day' account.

I had thought I was the brave one. Back then, I couldn't appreciate the courage it took for her to stay. She chose to do the right thing again and again. She fit her passion and her energy into a small, repetitive life for as long as she was needed there.

PEOPLE PERSON

Chapter Twenty

I can't remember when I first fell in love with her. It had been a slow-burning love. But since her mother's death, the nature of my love for Virginie had changed significantly. No less potent than before, I now couldn't question it, but if I thought about my love for her at all, I imagined a quiet temple with a powerful, low sound like a bell, and I gradually became aware that a heady, scented smoke had entered my chest. I was utterly overtaken by an intoxicating, healing, and cleansing perfume. Now, my system would clog and congest without it. A willing worshipper, I knelt and breathed from the censer that I knew would eventually suffocate me.

Irene had gone off to the loo again, so I took my chance to turn away from Annie and have a proper look at the old boy.

He was a dignified chap of about seventy and the oldest member of the jury. His see-through, white hair was beautifully clean, and the air around him was scented slightly with cologne and Imperial Leather soap. He wore a dark green, V-neck jumper over a sternly-ironed shirt and tie. He sat with his hands on his knees as if seeking support from the table before him would be shameful.

I engaged him in conversation while I had the chance.

Like all of us, he wanted to talk about the latest reports from the war. He was saddened by the deaths that had been on the news that morning, but he didn't question that the soldiers had been doing the right thing. He felt that it was a young man's duty to go and fight for the gentle and decent folk he had left at home. Just when I despaired of finding any common ground to begin my surreptitious persuasion, he let slip that he wasn't without criticism of the conflict.

"Poorly managed," he said. "No order, rushed in, and, um, under-prepared. That wasn't the old way. We used to rescue a people from an oppressor, then run things in a better way. We had the right to be in charge because we knew what we were doing."

Not my thing, but at least he was opening up. "Have you fought in many wars, sir?"

"Oh, yes. I had a general, name of Miller, who forever had to be seen to be doing something. He was responsible for the loss of more men than …. Well, not a true leader, you see. Sound bites these days. 'Tough on this and that.' What's your strategy, hmm?"

Damn, Irene was at the door. I did my best to block his view of her and gave him a winning smile. I had to move quickly.

"Oh, I know you can't say it these days," he went on, "but we got the basics right. If a country couldn't manage itself, we'd be on hand to advise, you know. Experience."

Dear God. Why on earth had Virginie chosen this old bigot?

Virginie's face swam before me. She had said, *"It would be too easy to put together a jury of people like us … easy and obvious. Too risky. I'd rather make use of the wrong ideas round here and change people's minds."* Saving herself combined with the greater good. Her plan was to create a mini-revolution of rational, secular democracy in the ignorant town she had grown up in, as surely as ripples on water.

I hoped I had got this one right. Had Virginie been here, she would have been the first to challenge Imperialist rubbish, but she had told me to use people's wrong ideas against them.

"And I suppose a parent could be like that, sir?" I said as quietly as I could. "In charge but causing such chaos and misery that it wasn't fair for them to run a household and be responsible for children?" He looked completely thrown, so I hurriedly explained, "I was just thinking of this case we've been hearing about. Some parallels?"

"Well, I must say, I can't bear the thought of a cruel mother. Now, it must have been particularly hard for a widow to cope, but she could have reached out to others for help …. Ah, hello, my dear."

PEOPLE PERSON

Irene sat down on his other side, and his gaze went straight to her. I left them in peace, beginning to feel a desperate sort of hope.

ALEX SPEAR

PEOPLE PERSON

Chapter Twenty-One

It had been a casual remark of her mother's that set it all in motion.

One day, she had said to her daughter, quite happily, that she knew that Reginald Pathaway would win the local elections.

"Only if enough people vote for him, Mummy," Virginie said through the pins in her mouth. She was repairing a large rip in the back of the sofa.

"Oh, no," cooed the Medusa. "He's much too clever to leave things to chance. He intends to be ... *proactive*."

"What does that mean?" Virginie turned to ask, her stomach giving a nasty lurch.

"Well, his son was electoral clerk until recently, and of course, he saw where the boundaries for the voting districts fell ... *so* biased towards a liberal party. All those blocks of flats where they believe in Nick ... so I'm insisting on a review of the boundaries. It just wasn't fair that all those voices weren't heard shouting at once for change."

Virginie looked at her mother in horror. She had just paraphrased one of Reginald Pathaway's slogans.

That was when we found out that a network of bigots was working at the town hall in the sleepy town of Swinton. It seemed worthy of one of her grandfather's conspiracy theories. The Keeping Britain

Great Party was planning to rig the local election, and the electoral records were at the heart of it. Virginie got her mother to admit that Pathaway's supporters had arranged another scheme to ensure he won the election. So many people in the area routinely didn't turn out to vote, and their votes were to be used discreetly for the odious man, thanks to the little gang of vote recorders working for him. With enough people in on it, the secret could be concealed. Postal votes for any other party would somehow never be received, and a surprisingly high number of ballot papers for the main rival, an earnest Lib Dem man, would be spoiled.

I later heard that the Keeping Britain Great Party had considered the whole of the country and flattered Swinton by choosing us as the area to infiltrate. There were some badly-maintained estates that occasionally flared into violence, and there were sufficient numbers of frustrated young men living there, who could be encouraged to blame their surroundings and tough lives on their black and Asian peers.

Jake, the confident juror, seemed to represent these men. I knew Jake would be the hardest, and rather than put off persuading him till last, I decided to make him my next desperate challenge.

He was dominating the room and most times seemed almost desperate for attention. This might prove to be an 'in.'

I got Jake talking. He had been showing off his leather jacket he got on a recent holiday to Italy. He was happy to tell me all about this trip as he had had an encounter with a hero of his.

"I met a *Mafia boss*," he breathed, eyes misty. "A don! A godfather! Can you believe that?!"

"What was he like?"

"He just had this ... presence, you know? Pure power. He wasn't all that tall or big, but he wore this huge, posh coat all the time, and I reckon he would'a had a good few guns under it, no problem.

"We were in this restaurant and my mate—I was visiting him, yeah, and he was the half cousin or something of the godfather's wife—so, we were there and then, they spot each other, and El Mafioso invites us to join his party at their table.

"There he sat, at the head of the table. And there was his wife on his right-hand side. She had so much respect for him. Well, she would do, wouldn't she? He had the money to look after her, all right. She was in all her furs and bling, and she was showing off the latest rocks he'd given her.

PEOPLE PERSON

"Their sons were opposite her, and the old man was telling me how they were going into the same line of work, and he was so proud of how they were shaping up. This guy could be hospitable, you know? He could just treat me and Alfie to this huge meal. He could get whatever he wanted. Free drinks all night, best table in the house and waitresses all over him." Jake had the same dreamy look as if he was falling in love.

"He could get whatever he wanted because he had connections. Power. Money. This man could have had anyone killed if he wanted. If you got in his way or didn't show him and his family respect, you were a dead man. Amazing. Amazing."

It was a tenuous link to the trial, but I had to give it a try. "Can you imagine someone getting in your way and you wanting them dead, then?" I shuffled the photos of Virginie on the table. "Like the woman in this case?"

Jake was confused by this. "No, I mean, like, *in your way* in a business way. You know? Like, you want to move a consignment of drugs from one end of the country to the other, but a rival gang's trying to seize it or some smart-ass cop's trying to cut himself a slice of the action–"

He sounded like he thought he was playing Grand Theft Auto or something. I interrupted, "What do you do for a living, Jake?"

"Bus driver. And the thing about this guy was that he was so cool, so calm, just loving being in charge of everyone. When you're the boss man no one can stop you, you know?" He finally looked down at the photos of Virginie. "She didn't have to go to those extremes. If you're not happy with where you live you walk out the door, you know what I mean?"

"But you can't," I blurted out. "You can't just walk away from your responsibilities." I hadn't meant to come across as so involved, but this felt important. I put my hand on his arm and made sure he was listening. "Can't you understand, Jake? That woman needs you to understand. When people you love are depending on you, you can't just take off and be selfish. You have to stay and go through whatever it is life has said you have to go through." I felt sick with my own hypocrisy.

"Easy, easy …" he shrugged off my hand. He was uncomfortable with me now. He was looking around the room for help. I suddenly realized all the other jurors had fallen silent and were staring at me.

Had I blown my cover? I was too worked up to care. This felt like a chance, and I had to take it.

"Listen, guys," I addressed them all. "I think this is the heart of the case. We must decide. Was this woman choosing to live like that: labouring every day, ground down by ingratitude, giving up everything she could have had to do the right thing? Does that sound at all likely? Because, if you think she was a prisoner, if you think she didn't have any choice, if you think she was born into a life of misery, then she had every right to take her life back. She didn't murder her mother. It was self-defence!"

After a long pause, Rita said slowly, "I do see what you're getting at. Yeah, I do see where you're coming from. You're saying she was almost like an abused kid …."

"Exactly. OK, she wasn't a kid. She was older, but she had never known any different than that house and that role. She was never allowed to become an adult, really."

Jake was bemused. "I thought we'd decided she couldn't lift the murder weapon?" he said. "It seems to me the girl wanted her dead and, one way or another, she or someone killed her. That's murder."

"Are we just forgetting the fact her mother was dying anyway?" Annie chimed in. "She might have been suffering, but we can't ask her now."

"No, there's another explanation for all this," Irene said. Others threatened to talk over her, but the old boy in the corner raised a hand, and we all listened to his new sweetheart obediently. "There's some other reason for all of this, I'm sure of it. It feels like there was some other reason why she was killed, and it's being kept from us. She feels like … a *pawn* … is that the word?"

I think I felt my heart stop.

PEOPLE PERSON

Chapter Twenty-Two

Virginie had run, giggling, into the canteen at uni one day.

Rachel shoved up to let her sit down next to us. I was sitting next to Charmaine, who I had met at meetings of the university gay society, which Virginie couldn't come to because it might get back to her mum. I had noticed the confident girl with the warm voice straight away, sitting right at the front of the meeting and regularly addressing the speakers.

"What's up?" I asked, cutting my Amaretto cheesecake in half, so Virginie could share it with me.

"Our envelope got delivered," she whispered.

"With the skunk seeds?" Rachel hissed. "Brilliant! Where are you going to grow them?"

"Can't grow them," Virginie said from behind her hand, still laughing. "Mummy must have thrown the whole thing in the fire. It was addressed to me, and she's burnt my post before," she explained for Rachel's benefit.

I nodded grimly. The Medusa had done this before in a temper. "But then–"

"Yes. They're ruined ... completely burnt, but the whole living room filled up with the smoke from the oils or whatever, and I think Mummy got a bit stoned! It was hilarious!"

"Oh, no!" Rachel and Charmaine were laughing now.

"Can you imagine? She was almost swaying when she walked, and she was slurring her words a bit. I hope she'll be all right."

"Serves her right for destroying someone else's post," said Charmaine. Charmaine was always beautifully dressed; she always covered her fat body in sumptuous robes and jewel-colored kaftans. She would often don a peacock-green satin turban with a diamante and feather arrangement at the front. Looking from her to Virginie was like looking from a bird of paradise to a sparrow.

"I can't believe she ruined thirty quid worth of skunk seeds," I grumbled.

"Cheer up," Virginie soothed, patting my leg. "Are we going to the town hall tonight?"

The Keeping Britain Great Party had been holding a series of open meetings at the town hall in which they would invite residents to complain about being ignored by the government and the immigrants they had heard about flooding into nearby counties. Then, Reginald Pathaway would stand up and create a mini manifesto in response to each story, explaining how every aspect of life would be better if the Keeping Britain Great Party were voted in.

Virginie always wanted to go. She said it was vital that anyone who disagreed with them went to their meetings and objected. I couldn't be bothered usually. She also wanted me to talk Mr. Patel from down her road into going as well. "The Keeping Britain Great Party says people like the Patel family should be sent back to India. He should come as well, so we can all tell them that's rubbish," she would say.

Mr. Patel had just laughed kindly when the young woman had earnestly explained to him why he should come to the meetings with her. "I've not got much time for politics," he said.

I agreed with this wholeheartedly. Life's too short to make trouble. I like being popular. Taking the line of least resistance had got me this far.

But his son was more interested. A fresh-faced lad of nineteen, Bobby Patel was excited by the sound of a public debate, and he said he would attend the meetings with Virginie. Born and bred in Swinton, engaged to a Swinton girl, and working in the Swinton branch of

PEOPLE PERSON

Vodafone, he was a great antidote to the Keeping Britain Great stance on sending all non-white people to their 'native' countries.

"I can't be bothered to go tonight," I said to Virginie, stroking her forehead. She was disappointed. "You go if you want. Come back to my place later."

"I don't think I can," she said. "Too much to do at home." She had eaten one forkful of my Amaretto cheesecake but could not relax enough to have any more. "I can't manage this."

"Can I have it then?" Charmaine said immediately, and after Virginie had gone, she and I shared the creamy plateful.

PEOPLE PERSON

Chapter Twenty-Three

When Virginie's grandfather died, she dropped out of university to look after her mother full-time. With the preparations for my trip, I hardly saw her. On her birthday, I went to the house, hoping to see her for a few minutes and give her the gift I'd chosen: a necklace with a slender, silver '21' on a chain.

Our days together before I left for Australia were growing fewer. I had booked a single ticket and planned to come back when I had run out of money. In the end, I was away for over a year. It proved too long for us.

Virginie was in her usual pose of labour at her stove. She was making her fresh onion syrup for our summer colds. Her hands shook a little as she held the honey jar over the saucepan. Why could she heal everyone around her and not nourish her own body?

"I got us some Strepsils," I offered, and she gave me a grin. I got them out of my bag even though I knew she wouldn't take them. She always had to do everything the hard way! Some old receipts and tissues fluttered out of my bag, so I screwed them up and stuck them in her bin.

I sat at her kitchen table while she worked. As I watched Virginie, another body, a healthy and fat body, wriggled before my eyes. For a moment I saw another woman, contorted in pleasure, greedily accepting anything I offered. Then, I was jolted back to reality when Virginie turned and her circular hipbones were visible above her jeans. Jesus. The skin was stretched over her pelvis as tight as a drum.

I knew my Virginie so well. I could virtually hear her mental monologue as she weighed out the oats for a medicinal skin scrub. Another half teaspoon would do it. The numbers on her digital scale crept up: 84g, 87g, then stopped triumphantly on 90g. I could almost see Virginie allow herself a moment's peaceful feeling of doing something right. It couldn't last though. Tipping the carefully measured 90g of oats into the saucepan, two delicate flakes were left behind in the scales. She looked pained as nausea filled her. She brushed them quickly into the pan with bitten fingernails.

I had to remind Virginie that she is an adult now and can do whatever she likes; however, any threat of freedom seems to push her more forcibly into self-imposed rituals. She had stepped on the bathroom scales the day before and told me apologetically that she'd lost another few pounds. Glancing down between her feet, I could see that this meant ten. I could hardly bear to touch her anymore. Thank God, the nights were getting colder and she was coming to bed in her faded blue pajamas. This summer had been a nightmare of her ribs and her huge horse-like hipbones. Her once delicate collarbone was now so sharply prominent you'd swear she'd broken it.

We still made love. I still loved Virginie. I wanted to be close to her ... until I was. When I held her tiny, fragile body, I felt I could break her, and the thought scared me. I held her and tried to give her some of the pleasure she could not take for herself. But I searched elsewhere, outside our love, for release.

Charmaine was one of the crowd coming to Australia, and in one of the most selfish choices I have ever made, I began my affair with her before we had even left the country together. We had nothing in common except the greedy, voluptuous sex we began to have in my room in halls in the afternoons when the building stood almost empty. She called herself a slut, and her dirty talk made our sex a simple, sinful transaction. With her legs wide open over my hip, she could shake her enormous bottom in the filthiest movement I have ever seen.

My Virginie was like an angel: remote, shining, and untouchable. On the stolen occasions we could make love—when we could be sure no one would work out we were a couple—she would take out pots of

PEOPLE PERSON

her herbal products to restore us. She would brush her long hair with a rosemary oil she had prepared from her garden. She would massage me with thyme or lavender and feed me her own rose hip syrup. In quiet moments, I saw her as radiant and healing. But the person she should have been and the person she had become, manufactured by that squalid childhood, were not the same. Her anxiety for order and self-control overshadowed the precious woman inside.

Virginie bent to the bin to get rid of the papery onion skins. In a horrible moment, I realized what I had just put in that bin, and my stomach was suddenly cold.

She was frowning and extracted the tiny piece of paper that puzzled her. "I don't remember buying …" she began.

"Virginie, I …." The right words wouldn't come. It was possible they didn't exist.

Virginie did not cry; she was too tough for that. But she shook slightly with righteous anger as she spread out the limp slip of paper on the table to read it. It was a receipt from a secret visit of mine and Charmaine's, to the indulgent café Virginie would never visit. It was dated the day before, when I had pretended to be too sick to come and see her, and had sworn blind I spent the day sleeping and sneezing. As Virginie's expression changed from confusion to anger as she realised what she was seeing, she waved the incriminating receipt in my face:

2 CSTD SLC
2 PAIN CHOC
4 CROISSANT
1 LRG SACH T.
2 PRESERVE
1 EARL G POT
1 DBL CHOC

"Who is she?" she hissed.
"She is no one, I mean, there is no one…" I lied, feebly.
"You're not telling me you ate all this…*rubbish* on your own…"
I had to laugh. "You are the expert in rubbish, my love, I mean – just *look* at this place. Can you blame me for wanting a little luxury?" I stopped when I saw the devastating effect of my hurtful words. I had gone too far.

"Just go," she said with more anger than she generally let herself express. "Go!" she shouted and ran at me, her hands outstretched. She gave me a shove but hardly had the weight behind her to hurt me, never mind move me. Shaking and crying with rage, she slapped and shoved at me until I fled her kitchen. She shut the door and must have thrown herself against it. I heard the thud and her sobs, and I slunk away.

PEOPLE PERSON

Chapter Twenty-Four

I wrote to her when I got to Australia. I tried to phone but hung up when I heard the mad voice of her mother. They had no internet connection and Virginie wasn't attending our university anymore, so email was no good. While the other students were emailing home, I wrote long letters and prayed they would reach her.

Maybe I was cruel to do it, but I detailed everything I saw and heard. I wanted to share the adventure with my Virginie, and in a slightly sadistic way I wanted to force her to understand what she was missing out on. Never having been in her situation, I was more of a child than she was, and I saw her refusal to leave home as cowardice rather than bravery.

My letters were the sneering, superior sort you write at that age. I was a know-nothing who thought I knew everything. My half-formed thoughts were scribbled all over sheets of my notebook, ripped out, and stuffed in a creased, reused envelope.

"I'm in Cairns now, which is like Ibiza, not that you've ever been ... tacky and full of English people ..."

"I can't wait to get into the red centre now. This is our most northern stop on the east coast, so from here we go slightly back the way we came, then west. I've seen enough beaches for a while! I wonder why I feel so at home in deserts. Maybe it's some sort of racial *memory, which I have dimly heard of. Perhaps we are descended from a tribe of desert people. Personally, I feel a bit crazy if I spend too long away from cities ....*

"Hooked up with an artist who's living out of his car when he's been round Oz. He's planning to go round the USA and paint the autumn foliage in New England. Such a good idea! I can't wait to see the results. I think a real painting just captures so much more than a camera ever could because an artist conveys not only what something looks like but also what it means to you at the same time, and an artist makes the viewer feel what they do. A photograph is so literal ...."

She never wrote back, of course. I had no permanent address, moving on to another hostel every few days. I looked at my watch on buses and in bed at night, calculating her time and imagining what she would be doing. Eventually, I stopped being proud and asked her to phone me, when she could, from the phone box at the end of her road.

"We're getting the bus to Townsville, after that to Mount Isa, then finally to Alice Springs, sleeping on overnight buses to save on accommodation:

MONDAY My time: 7:30 pm - 7:25 am
Your time: 10:30 am - 10:25 pm

WEDNESDAY My time: 7:45 pm - 9:25 am
Your time: 10:45 am -12:25 am (midnight)

SATURDAY My time: 3:05 pm - 11:20 am
Your time: 6:05 am - 2:20 am

I'll send you the number of the hostel we're in, and if you call me with the number of your phone box, I'll call you straight back, my Virginie. I miss you so much ...."

Leaving Charmaine in one of the backpacker pubs we were always in, I slipped away and moved heaven and earth to speak to Virginie on the phone. Call it lover's intuition, but I knew I had done enough to spur her to action, and though I was terrified of what she was going to say, I heard the echoes of it even before I dialed her number.

Virginie said she had read my letters and hearing about me living a normal, young woman's life had changed everything. She was filled

PEOPLE PERSON

with understanding that she would never be free while her mother was alive. Wherever she went, the guilt would go with her. Her mother's anxiety and the terrible burden of her guilt would never go away.

I didn't quite believe her. "Virginie, you've never done a thing for yourself, my love. Why now?"

I had a funny feeling she wasn't telling me her real motives. Of course, I found out later that this was to protect me and allow me to carry out the rest of her plan when she was unable to.

She explained it to me quite calmly. Virginie would brew her mother a herbal tea from the garden. She would say that she had incorrectly identified the leaves as those of Comfrey, a traditional tea; however, the coarsely hairy leaves in her garden were actually that of new foxglove. In the first year, there would be no flowers to give the plant away. She would give her mother a deadly tea of Digitalis Purpurea, also known as Virgin's Glove.

I was petrified by what she was saying. She was going to murder her mother. Me trying to force her hand and her resisting had been our status quo for so long, this sudden shift was like an icy blast of wind in my indolent life. I could only imagine what would go wrong and how she would be caught. To soothe us both, I think, Virginie told me some facts about her plant of choice. Her grandfather told her the plant had traditionally been associated with the virgin Mary, although this was likely a substitute for an earlier, pagan version of femininity, such as the Goddess Venus, altogether more sexual with hints of fertility and power. The foxglove, though deadly to humans and animals, was rumored to prolong the life of other plants around it.

I believed her when she said she planned to kill the Medusa as a bid for freedom, to save herself. I should have known this was a lie.

"If you must do it, don't do it that way, baby," I begged her down the phone. "Listen, you remember how we posted seeds back from Amsterdam? Let's do the same thing again …."

ALEX SPEAR

PEOPLE PERSON

Chapter Twenty-Five

The police arrested Virginie, mostly because there was no one else who could have killed her mother. The evidence was not conclusive, but Virginie had not denied the charge and seemed determined not to blame anyone else.

The Medusa had been found, vanquished at last, face down on the piles of her possessions. She had been dead an hour when Reginald Pathaway found her. Apparently, she had been hit on the head with a table leg but not particularly hard. The local police force were stretched for resources and didn't look too deeply at the case once they had made an arrest and had a working theory that was not disputed by the main suspect. The truth about the way the old woman had died was never discovered.

When I heard Virginie had been arrested, I put the next step of her plan into action. I couldn't communicate with her but prayed I had remembered all the details she had worked out.

I made my way to the Keeping Britain Great Party office on the edge of town. I knocked on the door below the small notice that read 'Britain for Brits.'

A little old lady answered the door. Her face was wizened, and she was so stooped she virtually peered up between her shoulders.

"I want to help the cause!" I shouted at her, not sure whether she could hear me very well.

"Oh, yes, dear. This way," she bleated and shuffled back in.

I closed the door behind me, trying not to dislodge the faded union jack that was draped across it.

She very slowly made her away across the dingy, carpeted hall area towards one of several doors. "Mr. Pathaway will be glad to see you, I'm sure. He hasn't had as much interest as he had hoped. He did much better in Birmingham."

She knocked on the middle door. I heard a muffled exclamation from inside. "A new member to see you, Mr. Pathaway!" she quavered. There followed pantomime noises of a man hurriedly packing things away.

After a minute, the office became quiet again, and we heard a sharp, "Come!"

I was allowed entrance. Mr. Reginald Pathaway, just as Virginie had described him, sat at a large desk, somewhat red in the face. I wondered briefly what he had been so eager to conceal, then wished I hadn't as grotesque and comical possibilities came to mind.

"Two teas," he barked at his retreating receptionist. She gave me a look and snorted with derision.

He was visibly outraged to be disobeyed. "Mother, I–" he began to protest, then gave up when he saw her expression of amused contempt. She shuffled off, and he irritably got up to close the door she had abandoned.

He had very shiny shoes. Virginie had briefed me not only on what he had said at the public meetings she had been attending, but also on his earlier views, which he had obligingly expressed in her mother's living room in Virginie's childhood.

I had gone to pretend to join his campaign. Virginie and I had always been very careful not to be seen together as a couple in public, and hardly anyone knew we were seeing each other. This had been to protect her mother's feelings, but ironically would now allow us to work together on the aftermath of her mother's murder without being connected. I hated all this lying and sneaking around, but it was the only way to stop the local bigots from getting their way. This would have pleased Pathaway if he had but known he was being outmanoeuvred in his own style. He was very keen on extreme measures being justified where they would achieve his ends.

PEOPLE PERSON

I said, "I wonder if I can be of any help to you?"

"Oh, yes. It's all women now," Pathaway smiled as though doing me a great favor. "Present company excepted, my dear, but it's all equality this and maternity that. Brussels interfering with an honest man trying to run his organisation and create jobs. I did have a girl here doing the filing, typing, cleaning, and making my tea, but it ended as I knew it would. She got herself pregnant, so I sent her packing."

"How did you manage that?"

"Oh, she was bleating about maternity pay—how these girls have the cheek to demand money for doing nothing is beyond me—but I said to her, 'You can have statutory if you sign a contract to promise you'll come back full-time. It's forty hours a week or nothing.' That shut her up. What's the point of women having jobs? Everyone knows they're going to get pregnant and leave." He got a misty look in his eyes. "How I long for a return to the days when a man ruled over his household and the wife was a cheerful subject: cooking, cleaning, and child-rearing. That's what I call *order*."

The scary thing was, I knew that Pathaway *was* married. I pitied his wife.

He asked where I lived and whether I wanted to hand out leaflets outside Swinton shopping center. I gave him a bit of flannel about why I believed in his cause. I parroted some of the rubbish Virginie had heard him spout at meetings: immigrants being the root of all evil, a return to the old social order of church, elitism, etc. I even gushed an imitation of a girl I had heard at one of his meetings: "What's wrong with staying at home? I *like* looking after my boyfriend!"

Pathaway had a peculiar way of switching off when anyone else was talking. As I spoke, he shuffled his papers, cleared his throat, adjusted his chair, and gazed out the window.

When he sensed the room had become quiet again, he seemed to come to and gave me some more information about his campaign. I found out a bit, just a few names of other Keeping Britain Great Party supporters in the area. It was enough to give Charmaine the leads she needed.

In the same way that the Keeping Britain Great Party had infiltrated local electoral machinery, we would do the same, ensuring that Virginie could exact her terrible judgement to prevent her mother from being a willing pawn. I would do whatever it took to keep Virginie out of prison, though I knew it wasn't as important to her. She would do what was right with a bloody-minded disregard for her own welfare.

He was off again. "Our country is threatened," he was saying quite seriously. "Our very way of life is under attack. There comes a time in a man's life when he must fight to keep the motherland from being gang-raped." He gave me a look of relish as he said this. "People round here don't want to have to fight for their own jobs against illiterate immigrants." He fumbled through his leaflets. "Do you know how much TB there is in the country now? It's all brought in by asylum seekers. Where is it? I can tell you the exact figure …."

"They have to go through awful things though, don't they, to seek asylum?" I blurted out, then wished I hadn't. Whoops. Had I blown my cover?

He wasn't listening though and carried on: "Oh, they're all bogus, made up reasons. They just want to live here and have their illegitimate children on our health service and claim benefits. Ah, here it is …."

He seemed to have found what he had been looking for, but then he continued to hunt obsessively through the paperwork on his desk. I cleared my throat to get his attention back.

"Er, can I help the cause?"

"Oh, yes," he lowered his voice. "Now, if you were a man, I would ask you to do a little job for us …. You haven't got a boyfriend, have you? Same sensible ideas?"

"Yes," I lied. "What should he do?"

"Patel family in the road where, er, that woman was murdered." He was careful not to let on that he had been to her house frequently, had made use of her influence at the council to gain a political platform for his vile beliefs and had rather suspiciously been the one to discover her murdered body. "The Patel son's a bit bolshie; been saying things at our meetings and could do with teaching a lesson. A few visits in the small hours would let him know he's not welcome. He wouldn't have to go on his own; a local boy called Mason takes a few recruits round to administer the 'lessons'."

"Anything else?"

"We had hoped to get a bit of support from the council in the run-up to the election … had a really 'good egg' on the inside, but unfortunately, she's no longer with us. Have you got any contacts we

PEOPLE PERSON

could use? Can't say too much about it, of course, but we'd like to get things going again."

It was all I could do not to gasp. I concealed the sharp intake of breath and fought to keep my face neutral. He was referring to Virginie's mother, surely?

"What happened to the 'good egg'?" I managed to ask, as if I had no clue who he meant.

"Asked a few too many questions. Became a bit too big for her boots." He suddenly remembered himself and gave me a sharp look. "What do you know about it?" he barked.

"Just what I've heard. No worries," I soothed. "I'll see what I can do for you, and I'll be in touch."

ALEX SPEAR

PEOPLE PERSON

Chapter Twenty-Six

Irene had brought up the subject of her divorce so often that it was easy to get her to talk about it.

"He just didn't listen, you know?" she was saying. "I used to be really confident, but after living with him for ten years, I wouldn't say 'boo' to a goose. It's funny how some people can make you feel squashed, isn't it?"

"Don't you think that's what happened in this case?" I angled. "A young girl having her confidence undermined by her mother had to break away?"

"Do you think so?" Irene sounded skeptical. "I mean, a man can bully you, that I could understand, but a frail old woman? She was quite a local do-gooder as well, wasn't she? How bad could she have been?"

I had to very carefully separate what I knew of Virginie's mother first-hand from the evidence the jury had been given. I leafed casually through the witness statements about Virginie's childhood. Hadn't social services been involved at one point?

I read aloud from the smudgy typed page. "Mr. Harper (grandfather of the defendant) presented at the local accident and emergency department with bruising to his lower back and legs. He said he had knocked over a pile of books at home and fallen awkwardly on them, and this had caused the bruising. He was slightly dehydrated and appeared to be suffering from early dementia symptoms but absconded before a thorough check-up could be carried out. Mrs. Harper, of the local council and a tireless campaigner for the hospital, was asked about her father's health and had said that he was in good spirits and there was no need for a home visit."

"See?" said Irene, relieved. "No need for a home visit. Things weren't as bad as the defendant made out."

Her casual use of the dehumanizing legal jargon chilled me. "That wasn't an expert saying that bit, that was the defendant's mother. As in, the deceased. She didn't want anyone to come round and see how bad it was, and she wanted to stay in control of her household. She may not have meant it, but she *was* a bully."

"You're living this, aren't you?" said Irene kindly. "Anyone would think you'd been there."

I couldn't speak.

"I think I know what you mean anyway," she patted my hand. "Let's see what everyone else thinks."

"Irene?" I asked wildly, trying to understand why Virginie had selected her for the panel, "Why did you divorce your husband in the end?"

Her face grew terrible and she said in a tight voice, "He started to treat our daughter as badly, and I was about to go along with it, because I was so under the thumb at home. I will never forgive him for that."

And she returned to sit beside her new friend, the old chap called Fred. He beamed at her like a little boy who'd just been given his own fawning puppy.

PEOPLE PERSON

Chapter Twenty-Seven

If Virginie had stuck to our plan, then what had really happened was this: In Australia, I made Virginie a birthday card, stuck glitter to the front, along with some foxglove seeds.

When their postman pushed it through the letterbox, Virginie's mother fell on it, ripped it open, and scanned it with malice. I had taken care to write 'I love you' prominently. It was proof of the imaginary boyfriend she had always known existed. She threw it in the fire as we knew she would. Then she settled down to rearrange her possessions on the floor right by the fire. I could picture her stewing over the interloper that would take her daughter away and obsessing over how to keep Virginie at home forever. But the room was filling with toxic smoke from the potent seeds. The fumes suffocated her. She fell and convulsed, banging her head three times on the table leg. Later, Virginie would put on gloves, carefully unscrew the table leg, and lay it next to her mother's cold, heavy head. Using a pile of newspapers, she was easily able to support the table without one of its legs.

I think that's what happened, but I couldn't contact Virginie after her mother's death. We had agreed that no one should know we had been any more than friends who had attended the same university course for a short period some time ago and hadn't been in contact since. We had been extremely *discreet* when we had been together, intending to save her family's feelings, and now, this would work in our favor.

Charmaine and I ran out of money in Australia and before long, the other people we'd come away with had gone off without us, continuing the adventure round Thailand. We were alone and penniless and homesick. I could hardly be bothered to have sex with Charmaine anymore. I didn't even like her all that much. But I couldn't go back to Swinton. Virginie had been arrested by then, and it was essential we weren't connected in anyone's minds.

Before my trip, I couldn't picture ever coming back, and if my mind had strayed to that future time, I had imagined that somehow, everything would be different. But in fact, I had learnt the irritating lesson that you can't run away from yourself. I was the same lazy, irresponsible person I had always been except now, I was five grand in debt and had destroyed the best relationship I ever had. When the very last of my money was gone, I begged the return airfare from my parents and before I knew it, I was back in rainy England and reluctant to go back to uni in September, but without a job or a purpose.

But now, Virginie needed my help.

I holed up with Rachel, who thought I just wanted to keep mine and Virginie's former brief involvement from confusing things. She believed that Charmaine and I were happy together. As agreed with Virginie, I let the investigation into the death of her mother unfold and heard second- and third-hand that Virginie had been questioned and then taken into custody. The case was confused by the discovery that the old woman had in fact been suffering from a progressive mental condition and had not been expected to live much longer anyway. That was when the whispers of a mercy killing had begun. Our gentle community had wanted to believe that a young girl could only undertake an abhorrent crime to spare her mother further suffering. The other rumour had been that someone else had done the deed and Virginie was taking the blame to protect them. Somehow, the thought of Virginie taking back her independence and fighting for herself was too shocking for our community to consider.

It wasn't until I had been back for over two months that Virginie's letter arrived. Her atrocious spelling had caused it to be misdelivered at first, as her version of my parents' address had taken a couple of goes for the postman to get her letter to them. My parents brought it round

PEOPLE PERSON

the next time they visited me at Rachel's. As soon as I was alone, I threw myself on my futon in the spare room and ripped it open.

Virginie's letter read:

2nd Sept

Hello Felix,

Forget about us, forget about the Charmaine thing, we can deal with all of that later. Please just make sure you cary with the plan as we agreed. You will do it all, won't you?

I've done it, and I don't know when you'll get this but its probabley the last time I'll be able to send a letter – the police have been round to ask me questions and they don't seem happy with my ansers, but they haven't said anything about taking me in or whatever they do. They will though.

I wanted to just explane why I did what I did. I know you think it's for me, but that's not quite true and I don't want any lies between us.

Why did I really do what I did? It was the worst thing in the world to do. Please don't think it was easy. I can't really explane properly without seeing you but basically it was for this area. It was for the people round here. The thing is, Mummy was in way over her head. I didn't tell you everything NP was asking her to do for him, on the council.

I love the people that live here, our little comunity, and I couldn't bare what Mummy and NP wanted to do. NP is always saying he is working for the local community, but really, he's working for himself and people that remind him of himself. With Mummy helping him, he could have done so much damage. She was the weapon, he was the poison. He would have made people that live in Swinton feel like they had to fight against each other. Make people feel like they were on oposing sides. Make people feel like we arent all the same.

It's a risk to write this bit down but – I need you to know that the seeds you sent, I intercepted them. I did it myself, a different way. I won't ever tell anyone how I really did it, even you. You wernt part of the act. Remember that. You are not to blame in any way.

Please cary on with the plan and I might have a chance. But either way, it's for the greater good.

Love, Virginie

I wasn't sure what she was saying about her intercepting the seeds was true. It was the kind of thing she would say, so that I wouldn't feel guilty. She had a way of always taking on other people's burdens. Had I killed the Medusa as planned? Had Virginie killed her as she said in her letter? Or were the gossips of Swinton right when they said that someone else had done it and Virginie was covering for them?

I should have guessed she hadn't acted for herself. A murder on behalf of the people of Swinton was much more her idea of justice. Maybe the fact her mother had been dying anyway made it easier for her to square it with her conscience. But now, if I could possibly keep her from prison and give her freedom at last, I would. I owed her at least that much. We all did.

Charmaine was working at the court and one of her mates was an official. He hated the Keeping Britain Great Party as much as we did, and she persuaded him to help us. The two of them working together made it possible to fix the jury selection.

Virginie had always said it would be too obvious to pick eleven people with views like ours to go on the jury with me. So, instead, she had carefully chosen individuals who seemed typical of Swinton residents but who each had either first-hand experience of killing a person or of a loved one killing a person. She hoped I could then influence enough of them to see the case sympathetically and not send her to prison.

It almost worked.

PEOPLE PERSON

Chapter Twenty-Eight

Jake voted himself as the person to deliver the verdict.

We filed back in the courtroom.

I knew what the verdict was, of course, but wondered whether Jake could resist spinning out his moment of fame and talking round all the conclusions the jury had come to.

"We find the defendant *not guilty*," Jake said, his face at first, funereal, then bursting into a broad grin when the courtroom erupted in gasps. "We believe the murder was done by Bobby Patel."

"Silence, silence, *please,*" the judge shouted over the general consternation. "I did not ask you for elaboration, Mr. Foreman."

Virginie had risen to her feet, and her face said wordlessly, 'No.'

"The defendant will remain seated," said the judge peevishly. Olivia gave a bitchy little simper.

I prayed Virginie wouldn't do anything rash. The jury had taken days to be persuaded that she hadn't killed her mother, and it wasn't my fault that they had latched onto the idea of a young man carrying out the murder. Bobby Patel was well-known to them all with his presence at Keeping Britain Great open meetings, which had been regularly reported in the local papers. He had argued with Reginald Pathaway about his policy to send Asian residents 'back' to India. It had been an easy leap in the minds of the jury to see the passionate boy as a criminal and his being from an Indian family had played no small part in this. Some of the jury had seemed to assume that he was a Muslim, and therefore a terrorist, despite my fierce objections to both ridiculous concepts. He was an atheist of Sikh parents and in addition I was keen to remind them all that it was a tough time to be a Muslim in the UK without us adding to the lies that Islam was the religion of criminals and suicide bombers. It seemed to make sense that a council member who had plans to assist the Keeping Britain Great Party was a potential target for a hot-headed youngster with a taste for politics. It wasn't ideal, but it was the best I could do to keep Virginie from going to prison.

In one way, you could say I did it for love. It was love that gave me the strength to do wrong. She had transformed me into a lazy kind of hero, but I was sick of love.

Sick of love and the way it makes another person more important than your own safety … your own sanity. I was prepared to sacrifice a young man's life for hers; sacrifice a person who had never done me any wrong just to keep her with me. I was sick of love and the flutter when you think you're going to see her. That was why I had run away from her. I was sick of love and the new family you want to create that makes you walk away from everyone else you loved from childhood. Maybe I wasn't grown up enough for love like this, love that made you feel duty and honour and loyalty.

Or maybe I didn't have Virginie's goodness. I was learning how much damage could be done when you had power without judgement.

Reginald Pathaway, sitting in the public gallery, was looking triumphant. This would add weight to his anti-Asian policies. None of the Patels had stayed to hear the verdict, thank God, but they would know about it soon enough. Presumably, the police would arrest Bobby and question him. I did not know whether they would find sufficient evidence to pin the charge on him, but I didn't care. I wanted Virginie to walk free more than I wanted to wake up each morning.

"Your Honour," Virginie was saying.

"Qui-yet!" the judge snapped.

"Your Honour," she would not be silenced. "I should like it noted that I can describe in detail how the murder was carried out. I know aspects of the killing that no one else will. I am prepared to submit further evidence to show that I was the guilty party and that I acted alone–"

PEOPLE PERSON

"Will you be quiet!" the judge roared. Both the policemen that flanked Virginie sprang up and seized her as if she had been throwing furniture around. They wrestled Virginie out of the courtroom, bending one of her delicate arms right up behind her back.

"Not guilty of murder but guilty of manslaughter due to loss of control was a possible verdict," the judge went on, irritated. "You have no business accusing other people who have not been tried. I did explain that to you, jurors." He turned to address us like a headmaster. "I thought I had made myself clear."

"Yes, but, sir," this was Rita. "She tried to take the rap, but that doesn't mean she done it, does it, sir?" Then she looked horrified by speaking out of turn and put her head down.

The judge was beside himself. "I declare a mistrial!" he screamed. "The jury is dismissed and will be replaced. Everybody out!"

The second jury took less than a day to find Virginie Harper guilty of the manslaughter of her mother. And just like that our plan had failed, and she was going to prison for a crime that many would have described as a public service.

She was sentenced to fifteen years.

ALEX SPEAR

PEOPLE PERSON

PART TWO

Why don't you weep
When I hurt you?
Why don't you weep
When I cut you?
You don't bleed
And the anger builds up inside.

"Brazen (Weep)"
Skunk Anansie
1997

"Your Honour, years ago I recognized my kinship with all living beings, and I made up my mind that I was not one bit better than the meanest on earth. I said then, and I say now, that while there is a lower class, I am in it, and while there is a criminal element, I am of it, and while there is a soul in prison, I am not free."

Eugene Victor Debs (1855 –1926)

ALEX SPEAR

PEOPLE PERSON

Chapter One

Virginie approached the lovely, old church, which had suddenly become visible beyond a bend in the road. Children in blue blazers were charging past her from the primary school opposite.

A mother and daughter scurried past, and Virginie could hear the little girl saying, "It wasn't fair. It wasn't even *me* that was talking …."

Virginie thought how lovely it would be to get married in the church they had been to every Christmas since they were little. Hugo would be coming back with a bride to the people who had seen him grow up. He would stand in front of the altar, tall and handsome, and show all the old people they knew from the village that he was a success. He was starting his own family now. Here was the beautiful girl who was to be his wife, and soon there would be children to go to the primary school with the hand prints on the sign.

Virginie had always loved the church—the huge, clean, clear expanse of floor and the perfectly constructed shapes of the stained-glass windows. But she hadn't been back for years as the things that were said there jangled in her ears, sounding as confused and untrue as some of the things her mother used to come out with.

The evening was very mild. She sat on a small, wooden bench outside the church, hidden from the main entrance by a large yew tree.

She loved the peace, the quiet, the gravel path, and the neat lawn providing a perfect meditation.

Patricia hadn't taken her eyes off Virginie. She circled slowly, never letting the bird-like woman hop too far away. She had agreed to remove the handcuffs and leave them in the pocket of her coat, but she knew that the large, plastic tag round Virginie's ankle would flash and scream into life if her charge made a sudden bolt.

Virginie made a short speech at the wedding, in which she recalled a story she had made up to entertain her little brother when they had been children. She was nervous about speaking in front of all their family and friends, and stood awkwardly, her head to the side, the toe of one shoe pointed and scrubbing at the flagstones of the floor. "Once, there was a girl who could only tell the truth. She and her brother were imprisoned in a horrible, ruined old castle by an evil witch and a mad old wizard. The wizard taught the girl how to make potions, but then he died. The witch was strangely controlled by an evil king in the area. The girl fell in love with a prince. The girl saved herself by killing the witch. Then the girl was imprisoned again and tormented by a monster who was really a beautiful mother under a curse. And the girl carried on telling the truth even though she was imprisoned. She was slandered, and the prince that she loved heard and believed that she had been untrue. But she managed to break the spell and turn the monster back into the beautiful mother she had been and set the other prisoners free in their hearts. Then, she escaped from the prison and returned home. The girl and the prince brought harmony and security to the kingdom, then they got married and lived happily ever after."

After the wedding, but before everyone had filed out for photos, Virginie and Patricia left the church. There was a lot of hostility towards her from the family after everything that had happened. Virginie allowed herself to be led back to the waiting car. Patricia put a hand on top of Virginie's elfin haircut as she got back in, out of sheer habit. She hadn't even bothered to take another member of staff out with her.

As Patricia started the car, she was suddenly aware of the enormous, brown eyes in her rear-view mirror. They were burning with thought and emotion. Animated by the conversations and pageantry of the service, Virginie stilled herself with difficulty and said nothing.

Patricia found herself avoiding looking in the rear-view, which was hampering her driving, and she swore to herself as she was overtaken

PEOPLE PERSON

by a motorbike she had not seen. Those eyes could not be ignored. They insisted on acknowledgement, communion. "Good do?" she found herself saying.

"Yes," was the best way Virginie could answer her captor, and they continued their journey back to the prison in a teeming silence.

ALEX SPEAR

PEOPLE PERSON

Chapter Two

You don't ask a woman what she did, that is the first rule. You usually don't have to, especially if it's one of the unpopular crimes that will result in retribution from the other women. One of the screws will usually give the game away, when a new woman arrives. When I first pitched up, the screw announced to the prisoners spitefully, "This is Twyla, and she is in for pushing drugs on little kiddies," so that they would all know what I had done and by Christ, my first few months were a hell of cigarette burns and razor blades in the sheets.

"Little kiddies" makes it sound like I was injecting babies with heroin, for fuck's sake. In fact, I sold pills and Charlie to the hatchet-faced teens in our block. My old man, Mason, got it all, in big bags of four hundred pills, and I'd divide them up and sell them on our estate. Enough people wanted them. Maybe I could have said no, but Mason's a scary bugger at times, and I've got no other way of making money apart from cleaning or going on the game. He kept it from me when we first got together. I'm not trying to make excuses. I'm just saying that was how we lived. I wasn't standing at the school gates; these were seventeen year olds and they came round our flat of their own accord. I'd been caught once too often, and this time, the judge lost his rag with me and said I was getting a custodial sentence.

Now, Mason can use me to sell drugs inside, too.

Most of the women are in here because of a man, one way or another. Why are we so soft and so stupid? Why do we do what they ask and end up being punished? I can't see Mason waiting faithfully for my fucking return. He'll likely have some slag round already. Probably Nicola Flint.

At least Vee made her own mistake. She didn't get banged up for anyone else. She's the quiet, little one who's just joined me in my cell since Maxine got parole. When she first turned up, she said her name was Virginie or some such, and I said to her, "That takes far too long to say, my love. We'll call you Vee," and now I hear her introducing herself with my new name for her. She tends to sit cross-legged on her top bunk, reading or just thinking. She looks like the Buddha on my clubbing T-shirt.

She's a dyke. There's a lot of that in a prison, of course. Women have their needs, and where there's no men, they turn to each other. I'm not like that though, so I hope she hasn't got any funny ideas about cellmates with benefits. I'd rather wait till I get out.

She got the usual first month of abuse and booby traps in the shower, and now, she's been pretty much accepted. She was lucky. Some women who've battered old people get the worst time. They're as bad as nonces, but Vee said her mum wasn't old or frail; she was just mental, and some people saw it as a kind of mercy killing. Vee's not up herself, which always helps. There's a couple of women in here who are fucking nutters. Like Lorraine. She's mental. You don't cross her, or she'd literally kill you.

Women in prison. We're mostly supportive of each other while we're inside. The friendships I've made in nicks have been some of the strongest in my life – it sounds funny, but it's true. But Lorraine and her mate, Leigh, are into smack, and that's what makes the difference. They'd do anything to make sure the drugs keep on flowing into the prison, so they've got their fix and they can sell them. They run the drugs in here, which means they run the place, in a way. For all I know, Lorraine might have been the nicest woman in the world before she got into smack, but now, she's either a monster because she's off her face on it, or she's a demon craving it who'll do anything to stay in charge. I guess she's desperate, but she seems in complete control. She always pushes newcomers to suss them out and let them know who's boss. If she doesn't like you, your life inside will be even more miserable than it needs to be. She's clever. She plays mind games.

PEOPLE PERSON

Take this week ... Lorraine had seemed like she was in even more of a foul mood than usual. Most of us sensed the danger and stayed well out of it, not speaking to her unless she barked a question. Tuesday, it all kicked off. Vee and I were in the TV room, which has got two knackered old TVs in it, one at each end. They're shit, so I don't even bother, but some of the girls have programs they never miss.

We could hear Daphne come flying in the front door. Daphne, by the way, has been to hundreds of meetings with social workers, especially that wet one from Access to Education, and now, she's got a piece of paper that says what we all knew—she is very, very slow.

"She lives for those kids," I said to Vee. "Daphne's said to me the only thing she was ever any good at was getting pregnant. But she's a lovely mum, even if she is a spanner. She's so kind-hearted."

The access times for prisoners with children never lined up with the times of the buses away from this vile place, so women missed out on precious time with their kids and were often late back and in danger of breaching the terms of their sentence, which was serious and could mess up your chances of parole.

We could hear Daphne trying to explain the delay, which happened every time, but she hasn't got the words or the confidence to get her point across. The screws are wankers, and we could hear them threatening to lock Daphne out if she was late back again, even though they knew full well it wasn't her fault. They behave like the worst bullies, the screws, and always want to see how much they can get away with. You have to stand your ground, but how can Daphne do that?

They finally got bored of humiliating her, and Daphne came barging in to the TV room. She sat down with us. "What are you watching?" she panted. She loved TV.

"I don't care. You choose," I said to her, handing her the remote. Vee's not fussy either.

A few of the women never miss Jeremy Kyle. Aytrisha, Lacey, and Fat Pat were sitting up the other end, about a foot from the screen. They really get into it and have big debates afterwards about the people on it and who was in the wrong.

Then, Lorraine came storming in the room, and we all went a bit quiet. Like I say, she'd been in a mood all week, and at that moment, she was clearly working out how she could pick a fight. She strolled up to the Jeremy Kyle group and pushed through them, nearly knocking

Aytrisha off her chair. She grabbed the remote and shouted, "This is fucking boring," and started flicking through the channels at random.

I tried to keep my head down and stay out of trouble. I ignored what was going on down the other end of the room and focused on our TV. Daphne was going through the channels painfully slowly, her face slack. "Hurry up and choose something, muppet," I said quietly.

Down Lorraine's end, Aytrisha and the others were complaining, but they didn't dare say much to Lorraine when she was like that. She gets a mental look in her eye, and then, it's just not worth getting involved. "What?" she said, turning from the TV and staring Aytrisha down. "You got something to say to me, bird?"

Aytrisha can handle herself, but she's not lairy. She said to Lorraine, "We were watching Jeremy Kyle, like always," but her heart wasn't in it.

"Get out of it, silly bitch," Lorraine said and she pulled Aytrisha's chair out from under her so Aytrisha fell awkwardly to the floor. She's done that to me before and it fucking hurts. She sat on the chair herself. She flicked through the channels, then turned the TV off. "It's all a load of shite," she said, then chucked the remote in the bin, so no one else could use the TV. She's just wild. She does whatever comes into her head and she doesn't care. The remote disappeared down under all the fag ends and Coke cans. She turned in her seat, looking round the room, just daring anyone to say anything.

Lorraine's eyes are a bit like a searchlight sweeping round. We could feel she was looking at us. Me and Vee sat quietly, hoping that Lorraine would get bored and leave us in peace. But Daphne never understands what's going on, and she went to the buttons on the TV itself, turned it back on, and began flicking through the channels, slowly taking in what each program was about. There was a loud click with each channel change as the dusty old buttons were cracked into life.

Lorraine suddenly screamed, "Turn that fucking TV off!"

Daphne sort of looked up, that stupid, puzzled look on her face but couldn't get what was going on and carried on clicking through the few options.

"Turn it off, quick," I muttered.

Daphne finally got it and turned the TV off, getting all flustered, and as Lorraine came marching over, Daphne had her hands behind her

PEOPLE PERSON

back and a guilty look on her face, like my youngest when he's done wrong.

It was too late though. Lorraine loves to pick on Daphne.

"That's it, you fucking retard," Lorraine said to Daphne. "I'm going to make you eat *humble pie.*"

There were gasps, and a couple of people said, "C'mon, mate," but Lorraine had got such a cob on that there was no changing her mind.

I saw Vee looking puzzled. "What did she mean?" she asked me when Lorraine had slammed out of the room.

"Hopefully, you'll never find out," I told her.

ALEX SPEAR

PEOPLE PERSON

Chapter Three

Vee got a letter one day, and I glanced at it over her shoulder. She said it was from her ex-girlfriend on the outside. All I saw was:

"… was so stupid to be unfaithful to you. I didn't have the guts to be with you only. If you are still interested, I would love to give it another try …."

"She sounds like a dick," I told Vee. "You're not going to take her back, are you?"

"I haven't decided yet." Vee looked sad. "She did hurt me a great deal, but we had a wonderful time together."

"It was only wonderful compared with the rest of your shitty life. Sorry."

Vee was only a newcomer, but she settled in quickly, and soon, she was taking other girls under her wing like a long-termer. She made friends with this young girl who came in recently, Whitney. Whitney was always crying. She was in for stabbing her pimp boyfriend. He didn't die, worse luck, and she was petrified of what he was going to do with her when she got out. She was coming off smack, so she was exhausted most of the time and either slept or just sat somewhere, tears rolling down her face. Vee would go and find her and sit quietly with her, listening to her thoughts about suicide and trying to talk her out of it.

"Suicide is a sin," Whitney would whisper over and over. "I'd go to hell." Then her face would crease, and her mouth would turn down even as she said it, and she was crying like she was already there.

Stabbing is such a personal crime. You need to be really close, literally at arm's length, and you reach out to the person and go for the heart. Reminds me of that time Mason tried to strangle me. It felt intimate. I looked at Whitney and thought, *I bet you any money you're still in love with him.*

Why are we so stupid?

Vee is a first-timer, there's no getting away from it. She's strong for other prisoners, but when she's on her own in our cell, she's just a first-timer: overwhelmed and sad. I see her sitting on her top bunk, lost in her thoughts, waiting. No one can prepare you for prison the first time. You're just waiting for it to be over, but it's your own life that's passing. You can never get those days and years back, and at first, you drive yourself mental thinking of all the things you're missing out on, like birthdays, anniversaries, kids growing up, and going down to the pub where your mates are, drinking and singing and just being together.

Forget what you've heard about prison being a cushy number. You do make friends inside, and you do look out for each other, but at the end of the day, it's an institution, and before long, you start to forget how to live in the real world. You end up like a load of bloody robots, controlled by bells and rules, and you forget that we've all been torn from separate lives, thrown together, and are all just waiting to be allowed out again.

PEOPLE PERSON

Chapter Four

I found one of my journals from that year away travelling. It was an expensive thing as I was so extravagant then. The front was tooled leather with a slot for a name tag, into which I'd slid a thick piece of cream card with the words, "Felix Travel Tales." I gave a sort of harsh laugh when I glanced through it. This is what I had to say:

"Travelling round Australia is an easy, safe experience for a woman, and I'd recommend it to anyone. You can crash in any hostel, make friends for a day or two, enjoy a restful day on the beach, go out for a walk in the bush, cook some Supernoodles in the shared kitchen, take a hot shower, or get some blameless sleep. Then, as soon as you're bored, you move on to the next town. If you don't drive, get a long-haul bus ticket from one of the companies where you can get off as often as you like. You can cover hundreds of miles on the bus overnight if you're running low on money and can't afford accommodation. Some of the backpackers might do a bit of busking, braid hair, or tell fortunes to make extra money, and some go fruit picking in the right season. By all accounts, bananas are the worst—Suddenly, a spider the size of your face will jump out!"

I had thought I was so clever.

Virginie now wrote to me about her institutionalized life in prison. Work a gruelling day in the laundry, go out for a walk in the garden, have your dinner in the dining hall, take a lukewarm shower, and get some fitful sleep. How similar our lives were, how unimaginative I realized I was. She gave a few details about some of her new friends and the problems that had brought them to prison. As ever, her anger was at the injustice, all the things in the world that needed to change to make things fair. Virginie always managed to come up with something to strive for, some way to work for others' benefit and improve herself. My goal was always to maximize my own comfort and minimize the effort I had to put into life. Her letters made me feel my youth and selfishness.

I went round to see Virginie's old house. She hadn't been allowed to inherit it, so it was sold off at a police auction. It was all boarded up waiting for the new owner to have it cleared and gutted. The rumor around Swinton was that it was a property developer who was going to convert it into tiny flats and rent it out.

Swinton's all about commuting. It's a soulless place with the entrance to the motorway, a failed shopping centre, and roads and roads of suburban houses. Adults like it because it's safe, quiet, and convenient for jobs; office jobs you reach via the motorway. There are also builders, plumbers, and electricians who've done well for themselves. Kids born round here can't wait to run away.

I broke the lock on the wooden side door and got into the back garden. Virginie's herbs were dry, overgrown, and woody. I found a watering can and did my best, but I didn't know what I was doing, and it looked a bit too late. Plants are delicate and respond to reliable maintenance and tenderness, and I've never been much good at either.

I pulled a few stalks of leggy lavender and crushed the dusty blue in my fingers. The scent took me straight back to those perfect days with Virginie. She had used fresh lavender in her bathwater and always had that subtle, medicinal scent, like cool air through an open window. What had her long hair smelt of? I ran around the garden, frantically pulling up stalks and stems, crushing each one to my nose. Finally, I found it. The tag on the woody bush read *Rosmarinus officinalis.* The rosemary oil I had first associated with her in our university love affair.

The scent conjured Virginie's ghost to me immediately, her shiny hair falling over both our shoulders.

The next time I went back to the house, the front door had a 'hard hats only' sign on it, and Virginie's garden had been surrounded by a chain-link cage.

PEOPLE PERSON

Chapter Five

Vee doesn't eat properly, not that anyone round here would notice. A lot of girls go off their food when they first arrive, but you soon get used to hearing, "You eating that?" and having the rest of your meal swiped by the woman next to you at the table. You have to be quick. But Vee doesn't seem to be *able* to eat quickly, so she just nibbles her way round a piece of bread while over half her meal gets stolen. She can't afford to lose any weight either. I did ask her about it, but she just smiled and said something like, "Oh, I'm tougher than I look. Please don't worry about me."

At least she makes an effort to eat something. Little Whitney just cries all the time and doesn't eat at meal times. She's looking ill, and her skin, which started off like my Aubergine Diva nail varnish, is a scary, greyish colour now. Virginie will sometimes sit next to her and offer her little pieces of bread, like she's feeding a bird or a kid. One night, I heard Whitney saying between bites, "I just don't think life is for me, Vee."

Vee said, "Do you think we have that choice? Isn't it our duty to live?" Which is sort of what I believe, but I would have never thought to put it like that.

I know Vee would have loved a job in the prison garden, but they keep those for trustees, women who've been here a long time and suck up to the screws. Instead, she got one of the classic dirty jobs that everyone does for a stint when they arrive: laundry duty. Soon, her shiny, short hair was lank and dull. The grease and the steam seem to get into your pores and under your fingernails. Girls who work in the laundry can never get clean. She was strong though, which you need to be to pull the heavy, wet washing in and out of the different machines. And she never seemed to mind it, somehow. She just set her jaw and got on with it. The laundry is a grimy, soul-destroying place, but Vee's a good girl. She seemed to get some grim kind of satisfaction from getting the work done, making a clean and practical product from dirt and confusion. Just as well, because if you can't find something to occupy you while you're inside, you'd fucking top yourself.

One night, about a week after Daphne had pissed Lorraine off, we woke up to hear it all kicking off in the cells. We could hear women shaking things: keys, lighters, jewellery—making that funny, high-pitched jingling noise that makes my stomach turn now I have come to know what it means.

Retribution.

Vee whispered from her top bunk, "What's going on?"

We heard the key turn in our door lock. Someone was letting us all out. I reached up, took Vee's hand, and helped her down. "Easy. You don't want to take a tumble in the dark. Now, come with me and don't make a sound."

We ran along the corridor, joined by others, till we skidded and stopped at Daphne's cell. There was light inside ... a torch. Women were crowded in the doorway and more were on the bunks.

Poor Daphne was sitting at the table, retching over her humble pie. Lorraine had hold of her hair and was hissing, "Eat up," in her ear. Lorraine's mate, Leigh was shining the torch in Daphne's face, so we wouldn't miss any of the goodies she was being forced to chew and swallow. Fox shit was the favorite, there being so much available in the gardens and it being disgusting and toxic. Legend had it that a woman died in the past from a fox shit humble pie.

Lorraine took a handful of the brown mess and smeared it over Daphne's lips. "Open up!" she scream-whispered.

PEOPLE PERSON

Daphne's face was wet with tears, sweat, and snot. She gagged and shuddered for breath, and Lorraine took the chance to poke a shit-covered finger in her mouth.

Just then, there was a voice. *"Stop it!"*

Oh, my fucking God.

The torch swung round the faces. Everyone had gone from looking excited to terrified.

Lorraine properly screamed this time. "Who said that?"

It was clearly Vee. She was shaking and still had a finger pointing at the scene.

"You can't do that to her, Lorraine," Vee said, almost in tears. "Draw the line!"

Lorraine seemed like she was going to laugh. She came towards Vee, and the huddle of women in the doorway fell over each other trying to get out of her way.

"Little girl, you show me respect, or you'll get the same treatment," Lorraine said quietly.

Leigh grabbed Vee and hauled her into the cell.

I couldn't just leave her. "C'mon, Leigh, mate, she didn't mean it–" I began, but a punch in the face soon shut me up.

Vee stood in front of Lorraine and said, "I'd rather you made *me* eat it and leave Daphne alone. You know, she didn't mean to 'dis' you. There's no harm in her." Vee was sounding like one of us. I would have been impressed if I hadn't been shitting a brick with fear. But then, Vee went too far. "You don't care who it is, do you, Lorraine, so long as you get someone to play with?" With that, Vee, who seemed like she'd gone completely mental, shoved Daphne out of the chair and sat herself down. "Lorraine?" Vee said, and then we realized she was serious about it.

It was like a nightmare. Was the girl tripping? She was asking to be force-fed someone else's humble pie. Lorraine seemed like she didn't know what to do, but she soon recovered.

"All yours, skinny cow," Lorraine said, and smeared a handful all over Vee's face. Vee had clamped her mouth shut, and I could see none of the muck had got in ... yet. I was so scared for her.

But the mood of the women had changed now. We all knew you didn't mess with Lorraine and Leigh, but at the same time, something about this just wasn't right. It wasn't *her* humble pie. She hadn't done anything to deserve it and the wild kind of excitement had gone as cold as a witch's tit. It wasn't *right*.

A couple of women sort of complained, and then a few in the corridor drifted back to their cells, and then, the shout of "screws" went up and everyone went back to their beds. I couldn't go without Vee, but I could hear the bunch of keys at the lock on the main corridor, and I knew we had seconds to move.

Lorraine gave Vee a last punch in the head, hissed, "Watch your back, dyke," and ran off. I grabbed Vee and shoved her down the dark corridor, trying not to let either of us run into anything. The last thing you want to do is knock yourself out and be lying there unconscious when the screws come running in. Some wouldn't be above stamping on you in the dark.

We reached our cell, and I shoved Vee back into her bunk, then threw myself down on mine. Our door was closed but unlocked. If our cell was searched and Vee was discovered with her face smeared with shit and both of us dripping in our own blood, we'd both earn some serious time in solitary, and I didn't fancy that for either of us. Saying that, and remembering how Vee had undermined Lorraine in front of everyone, I realized solitary confinement might be the safest place for her for a while.

PEOPLE PERSON

Chapter Six

I wrote to Virginie constantly, begging to be allowed to visit her. She had had to stay in a Category A prison initially, but after such good behavior, she had been moved to the current prison with some scope for regular visits.

I'd been restless when travelling, and now that I was back, I felt bored with any other company than hers. I realized how stupid I had been to wreck our relationship. I had not wanted to miss out on being young and free, but the truth was, I had thought about Virginie every day since we first met. I had gone searching for an elusive perfect relationship and perfect life when, in fact, we had been perfect for one another. I was still hopelessly in love with her, and life was hollow without her.

She wrote back a bit about life inside but always ignored the visiting question. I had known that she would consider the situation, then either decide that it was impractical to ever forgive me, or she would rationally conclude that it was worth us trying again. Last week, I received a letter from her that made me punch the air. It was a page of yellowed, prison notepaper, which simply said:

"Yes. Visiting day is this Saturday, times 10am-12 noon. Please could you bring me a warmer jumper?"

The grounds of the prison were set with a thick frost. A coach had collected all us husbands, partners, and children from the station. We walked the short distance from the coach to the gates and up to the main door in silence. It was too cold to talk, and we had said all we wanted to on the coach. I was beginning to learn that there is a special depression that settles over a family whose woman is in prison. With her gone, a home seems to lose its fire from the grate.

Weary men, bewildered children, and staunch mothers filed in. We sat at stained, plastic tables. When we were all settled and the prison officers felt they had control, they let the prisoners come in.

Virginie was one of the last to appear. She had lost some of her energy, that much I could see. Her walk over to my table spoke of a lack of vitamins, fresh air, and joy. She smiled when she saw me, but her forehead had fine lines over it I hadn't seen before, and her cheeks were pinched and drawn.

I stood up as she walked over. I pressed the jumper I'd brought her into one hand and money into the other. "My first pay packet. It's yours."

"I'm glad to hear you've got a job, Felix, but keep your money," she said immediately, pushing it back. "I make my own wages in here. It's sufficient."

I was chastened. She was rarely impressed by my grand gestures, but I think we both realized that the old magic was there. Virginie adversarial, pushing my hand away, me running an eye appreciatively over my fiery, difficult woman. Our gazes locked, and suddenly, it was very difficult to concentrate.

"When do you get out?" I asked, my brain muzzy with desire.

"I could be halfway through my stretch," she muttered like a proper convict. "I could do less than six years, parole, good behaviour. I've got a social worker. She's quite helpful. We've discussed *strategies*." She ran a hand up my sleeve, and I winced with the familiar sensual excitement she caused in me. She still seemed to have the direct route to my ... Well, I don't have to spell it out.

"What's the maximum you could be in here for?"

"My full term—fifteen."

Fif ... Teen.

Years.

I had heard it in the courtroom, of course, but that all seemed like a bad dream now. How could that be right? She had been in her early

PEOPLE PERSON

twenties when she went into prison. She could be nearly forty before she got out. You don't get that back again. The best years of your life, your most free, your most your own. Gone, swallowed by a grim institution, spent alongside the vicious and the exploited.

She had that defeated look again. I had to say something to get her through this. I babbled, "Virginie, listen to me. When your mum was alive, you told me you'd never be free till she was gone. Now, she *is* gone, and you made it happen. I know you're locked up and you've got to mark time for a while, but aren't you freer than you've ever been? Can't you choose to be free? Isn't free a state of mind?"

It was like one of my grand gestures, optimistic yet hollow, but she gave a cynical little laugh.

After a while, she said, "I've waited longer than this for my life to begin."

"So, you'll wait a little longer. Can you find stuff to do while you are here?"

"Supposing you're right and I am free here, how does that add up?" She was into her logic now, which I could never understand. I waited for her to come to the correct result, which was the one where everything was squared off and she felt satisfied. She was making it true in her mind, like an equation. "I *am* free. I can think and be still, and I'm not surrounded by any kind of clutter here, that's for sure … and when I work, I work for *me*."

"When I work, it's for you," I tried to suck up, hoping for some praise, but she was busy with her thoughts now.

"And while I am here, there's a lot I want to change," she said with the familiar fire returning to her eyes. "The way the women are treated when they have a baby, for starters." She leaned in and dropped her voice. "I think Lorraine's pregnant," she whispered.

"Which one's Lorraine?"

"Don't look now! In the corner, long hair."

"Hard as nails with the young lad?"

"Yes! He's her partner's son from his first marriage. I hear all this gossip. Isn't it terrible? No one's life is a secret. Lorraine always seems so angry. I'm glad she's got someone visiting her. Her partner never comes. He's ashamed she's in prison. No one thinks he'll wait for her."

"Which one's your cellmate? Twyla?"

"Not here. Mason hasn't come to see her. He's taking some drugs somewhere. Apparently, he's driving a car across Europe with a big bag of pills in his pants."

"My God, it's all going on in here. Don't you become a hardened criminal."

Looking back, I still can't believe Virginie never told me about the hell Lorraine was putting her and the others through. I wish she had shared it with me at the time, but she never complained. Maybe she had absorbed the culture of prison, which dictated that squealing was not permitted. Maybe it was because she saw herself as lucky compared with some of the other women.

"That one over there is Daphne," Virginie continued. "She's been inside twice for housing benefit fraud. She's got countless convictions for it, and eventually, the judges want to make an example of a repeat offender and put them inside for a bit. What's the point?" Virginie was angry about this one, I could see that. "It's a woman's crime and a crime of poverty: fudging a form about how many children you've got living with you, how many wage-earning adults, and ignoring how many people are doing work cash-in-hand. You screw the government out of a few hundred pounds, so you have a bit more to spend on your family. What a lot of people don't know is how wasteful government departments are with that money. I saw that through Mummy's work on the council. What do I care if Daphne has a bit extra? How else is she going to make money? And who has she really harmed?"

"I don't know, my love. You're beautiful when you're angry."

Visiting time was almost up, and we visitors were being sheep-dogged back to our coach by the stupid, cunning-looking guards. "Look, I'll work," I said desperately to Virginie. "I'll build up a home and a life for us. Just promise me you'll come back to me as soon as you get out of here."

"You'll wait for me?" Virginie looked skeptical. "Well, I might join you when I'm out. We'll see if you deserve it." I loved her teasing. Then a burly uniformed woman walked in front of her, arms out to the side, and my Virginie was gone.

PEOPLE PERSON

Chapter Seven

The funny thing was, Lorraine kept making threats about what she was going to do to Vee, particularly when there were others around and Vee was in earshot. We passed each other in the corridor, and Lorraine would shove me and Vee against the wall and say, "I'm going to give that dyke something to smile about, don't you worry about that. Enjoy eating your dinner while you can, cunt." I didn't want to tell Vee what that meant. A Chelsea smile is almost as frightening to think about as it is to get.

But as the days and weeks passed away, we realized she hadn't done anything. And Vee said the one time they'd been alone together, and Vee was convinced she was about to be annihilated, Lorraine hadn't lifted a finger or even made any threats. It was weird.

Eventually, we breathed more easily and just prayed Lorraine had moved on. Vee got involved with teaching Daphne and some of the others to read and write a few words. She'd get me to check her spelling first because she knew hers wasn't the best. She'd grumble, "When people are dependent on *me* for writing lessons, they must be desperate." She thought someone else should be offering prisoners like Daphne an education while they were inside. There was a bit on offer we'd heard of. A mousy, little social worker used to appear once a month and bleat on about rehabilitation, but there wasn't much for someone as slow as Daphne; she needed someone to be extremely patient. Vee gave her the time because she was worried that Daphne had a lot of debts on the outside, and she wanted her to be able to read the letters from the loan companies before she signed her life away. Daphne's kids were at her mum's, and she was looking forward to being able to write them a proper letter. Someone would always write it for her with her dictating, but sometimes you want a bit of privacy with your family, don't you?

Vee got clever at the things we do. She's a right lag now, with the best of us. Take meal times ... According to Fat Pat, who's been here forever, it used to be prisoners who worked in the kitchens. If your mate was on duty you might get a bit extra, but so much food was going missing. Now, they were cutting costs and so instead it's these 'kitchen helpers,' which always makes me think of Charlie's Angels except they're not very angelic. Grumpy jobseekers on some programme; none of them want to be here, any more than we do.

Anyway, these kitchen helpers are in charge of doling out the food we eat, which is quite a big deal inside. Don't get me wrong, it's all muck—watery white sauce with an occasional scrap of chicken or miserable pasta bows with boiled carrots and a few bits of mince like sawdust—but if you don't get a decent amount, you're starving all day, or worse, all night. Luckily, the kitchen helpers are thick as shit and easy to confuse.

One dodge was for two women to work together. One would make sure she was at the front of the dinner queue and get, say, her baked potato with beans and cheese. To ensure the maximum number of kitchen helpers had a job, they had us prisoners queue up for the spud, then a different kitchen helper would dish up a meagre helping of beans and a third would sprinkle on the meanest amount of cheese. But what you'd do is, once you'd got to the end you'd wolf down your topping and then take your naked potato back to where your mate was queuing in between the spuds and the beans, and you'd rejoin the queue next to her. Then you'd get your potato re-topped with the good stuff. Of course, you'd return the favour for your mate, and they'd go round again while you queued up for them. The kitchen helpers didn't look too closely, and if you disguised your appearance a bit by quickly tying your hair up in a ponytail or shoving on a baseball cap, you could go

PEOPLE PERSON

round three or four times and get a really decent meal out of the fuckers.

Another dodge was to make the helpers miscount. They've always got more food in the kitchen than they give out to us because they want a load of leftovers for themselves and the screws. One day, glory be, it was doughnuts for afters, and we all wanted two. They had us sitting at tables of ten with one screw assigned to each in case we attacked each other with a plastic fork. A few of us went up and said, "We'll take them for the whole table to save time. Give us ten each." The helpers were skeptical, but that was the genius. They thought each of us was going to keep the ten for ourselves, and the other women's beef would be with us, so what did they care? While the helper was counting out ten, one of us would look her dead straight in the eye and say, "Have you had your hair done?" or once, someone at a table jumped up and ran through the kitchen door and made the helpers go after her for a second. Either way, the one counting would forget whether she'd got to 'six' or 'eight.' You'd be standing there with eight doughnuts, but your mate would have quickly taken two off you and ducked behind the counter in the split second the helper was distracted, so the helper would count up what you were holding, "One, two, three, four, five, six," and give you another four. That's two extra for your table—one for you and one for your mate. They may have been mean and aggressive but thank Christ those kitchen helpers were not bright and were more gullible than screws. That's the only way we got a good feed.

Some of the women went in for 'steaming,' where they'd crowd up behind and in front of a woman who'd got her dinner or a something from home and pinch it off her. But there's no honour in tricks like that. There are things you don't do: you don't squeal to the screws, and you only cadge food from the kitchen, not from other prisoners.

Vee was happy enough to do her fair share of nicking extra food, and she never seemed to want her full portion either, so she became quite popular. Even without parcels from home, she always seemed to have so much to share.

One day it was some apple pie for pudding—all greasy pastry and a little pile of chunky syrup that might have once been apples—but it came with squirty cream, which we all wanted more of. The kitchen helper on squirty cream duty was giving each portion a mingy little rosette. She barely had her finger on the button long enough to make the nozzle start to hiss before she was finished and on to the next one. Mean cow! It wasn't like she didn't have enough to do us all. She had another three canisters standing by on the counter. Vee and I were standing there waiting for ours, and then, in a moment of genius we all talked about for years, Vee said in her innocent voice, "Oh, look. Is something on fire on the stove?" and pointed behind the cream woman. It was enough to make the woman turn, and quick as a flash, Vee swiped one of the canisters and pressed it under the counter into my hand as I was leaving! Oh, we celebrated that one all right. Vee was carried through the cells at head height while we all took turns to squirt cream straight into our mouths. It tasted all the better for being nicked, I can tell you. With a shock, I realized that Vee was looking quite attractive. Where did that come from? I never thought about a girl being all kind of heroic and sexy. That short, shiny hair doesn't help either.

It's mad that grown women can become so excited about an extra doughnut or a canister of fucking squirty cream, but it's about getting one over on the system. It's a way of keeping your sanity. You can't bear the thought that you're helpless, that you have someone else telling you when to go to bed and when you can see your family, so you take back control in these stupid, petty ways. Once you've been locked up, it makes perfect sense.

PEOPLE PERSON

Chapter Eight

On the outside, Virginie haunted my thoughts. She had always been something of an inspiration to me. She was like my conscience, and as the years went by, I heard her voice more loudly in my ears and more often.

I resolved to make myself the person she would want to be with if she ever got out of that place. She was practical as well as romantic. I needed a steady job and a home for us both. Rather than run away travelling, this time I would learn from her how to stay and go through the mundane aspects of life as well as the fun.

I had abandoned my degree and had no training or experience, but I had my passion for food. I tramped round every restaurant in Swinton offering myself as a short-order cook. None of them would have me. But at the very last I tried, Chariot, the bottle-washer had just walked out. The job was mine if I would work cash-in-hand for less than minimum wage and keep my mouth shut.

I knew how Virginie would have responded to this. Setting my jaw, I washed up.

It was the hardest work I've ever done. The pressure in the kitchen of a restaurant is unbelievable. Every night I would go home exhausted but too wired to sleep. The heat, the noise, and the demands are like nothing else. All day and evening long you've got people screaming at you, different words but always the same message: shape up or ship out. You must be seriously tough to stick it out. You need to stay confident that you are good enough and you deserve your place there or you'd crack.

At the end of the night when the place is shut down and we've done all the cleaning and prepping down, we eat together round a buckled cast iron work surface near the doors. We eat whatever's left over. It's not the shared, nurturing meal of a family exactly, but there is a certain grudging respect in the silence. There's a sort of unspoken acknowledgement that we've all lived through another day's service and survived.

PEOPLE PERSON

Chapter Nine

Most evenings I would wait for Vee to finish in the laundry. She always liked to organize the bottles of bleach, detergent, and powder at the end of her stint. "Leave it," I said to her. "Someone else coming on shift can deal with all that. What do you care?" But Vee did care. No matter how long she was in the system, nothing could make her lose her pride in her work.

When she finished, we went out to the garden. We tried to get out there as often as we could. She loved to be near the trees, just stand on the grass and 'drink in' the little areas that trustees had cultivated. Women maintained a few scrubby flower beds and had a couple of plots of vegetables that sometimes did all right on the thin, dusty soil. I laughed at Vee at first for being so keen to get out there, but I must admit we both look fresher when we come in from a spell out there, just looking.

There's a groundsman we call Mr. Peterson, who's often seen out there cutting the grass or wrestling equipment in and out of sheds. You have to padlock everything portable, even twine and chain-link, or some woman will have it. We don't even want the stuff we half-inch, it's just the principle. Mr. Peterson has several seasonal lads who come and go to give him a hand, probably lags themselves. Hard as nails most of them and not above groping a girl as you go past. Some of the women love it and no doubt get up to all sorts behind the sheds when Peterson and the screws aren't looking. Personally, I can't think of anything worse than a quick leg-over behind a tree with the gardener's lad, like a bloody dog. But I suppose a woman has needs, and some of the younger men hadn't been bad looking. I don't judge ... but honestly.

The current groundsman's assistant is the worst we've had. He looks like a nonce or a serial killer. Alf, he's called. He's not all there, you can see that. Over seven feet tall, small dead eyes, strangler's hands, and he's got a horrible, high-pitched voice. None of the women cozy up to him.

Last night, Vee and I were standing in the lovely red sunset, looking at the gardens when Peterson and Alf went by. Alf suddenly fell on something and pulled it up, grinning and shouting. It was a huge mole wriggling to be free of Alf's massive hands.

Alf held it up to show us, then snapped its neck. Just killed it right there without a thought. It turned my stomach. Alf waved his trophy round by the tail, gesturing and shouting, childish delight all over his grown man's face.

I pulled Vee back indoors with me. She felt cold and her face looked like I felt.

Vee hasn't been at all well this winter. She keeps getting coughs and colds and not getting over them properly. I've told her she needs to look after herself because no other bugger will in here. I told her to her face that she was working too many hours in the laundry, trying to save up money for when she got out. Most women work inside to pay for fags and little things like shampoo, things that make you feel human. You earn a pittance, so it doesn't buy much more than that. But Vee didn't smoke and seemed to need less stuff than a nun. She had this plan that by the time she was out, she was going to have saved enough to put down a deposit on a house. None of us had heard of anything like it. None of us owned anything; it was enough trying to scrape together the ready cash for things we wanted right now. She'd worked it all out. Six quid a week she could put away, meaning that each year she had to stay in this place, she was three hundred quid closer to her deposit. It was like getting one over on the system on a huge scale. The longer they kept her in, the more they were helping her out. Sometimes, you have to kid yourself like that otherwise you'll go

PEOPLE PERSON

mental. She reckoned she still had some savings too, if the police hadn't frozen her account.

But this weekend, she had clearly worked herself into the ground. She was dripping with sweat, paler than usual, and couldn't get out of her bunk. I went round and bashed on the screws' common room until one of the lazy fuckers agreed to phone for the nurse. An hour later, the nurse was in our cell taking Vee's temperature. Vee could hardly hold the thermometer in her mouth and her eyes kept closing.

"Nearly 38," the nurse said. "Better stay there today."

"Aren't you going to take her to the san?" We called the miserable little room for sick prisoners the 'san.' Don't ask me why. It smelt of witch hazel and piss, but at least you could go to sleep in the middle of the day and not have some joker drawing on your face.

"San's full," the nurse said without much pity. "Too many malingerers in there already. You," she said, tapping Vee's forehead with a finger, "drink more water and give up smoking, then you won't look so pale."

"Vee doesn't smoke," I protested.

"Well, then, tell her to be pickier about what she eats. You women love to eat rubbish, I know." The nurse was already down from the bunk and grabbing her bag. A magazine slithered out, and she tucked it back in. "I'll see how she is on Monday. Now, you," she poked my head this time, "outside in the fresh air before the germs get you too."

Do you reckon she's even a real nurse? I've never heard of one so uncaring. "Is it too much to ask ..." I couldn't think of the right words, "... to be made a fuss of when you're feeling really ill?" I had raised my voice to a member of staff, which was always stupid, but I couldn't help it. I was so annoyed for Vee. "We're still people, you know. All we want is a bit of *care*–"

"That's enough out of you. You're about to earn yourself a week stuck in your cell for 21 hours a day. Is that what you want?" She was perfectly calm. Why shouldn't she be? All the staff backed each other up. She could get any punishment dished out. "Now, get outside."

"You need anything, you bang on the window, babe," I said to Vee as I went out.

In the garden, I mooched about, smoking a roll-up. Aytrisha said hi and was wandering about nearby, keeping an eye out for screws, probably smoking a reefer. Weekends were the worst: no work, no structure to make the day pass more quickly. There was just "outdoor activity" where we're supposed to get exercise and shit like that. Lacey's been in a category C prison, and they had a gym, but there's nothing like that here. Our prison buildings are two hundred years old. There's just the grounds and a big wall. Being left to our own devices makes the time pass even more slowly than usual.

It's not calming either. It's not like you're whiling away the time peacefully. You're constantly on edge because you have to stand your ground about everything or some fucker will walk all over you. You can't ever let your guard down and just be a person. You must be hard twenty-four seven, and it grinds you down.

You think about the other women constantly. I might as well be a lezzer while I'm in here. I wake up in the night obsessing about Leigh and her latest aggression. I go over and over in my head how I should have stood up for myself, or worse, I review the guilt-stained memory of how I did stand up for myself. I remember how I snarled, how I used my words to maim, how I used my nails to twist her skin under the arm where the screws can't see.

The tension of it. I wake up at 3am or 4am most mornings, and as the sick light creeps in and turns the corner, it's Lorraine's face I see, and I relive her moods, her whims, her orders. I grow hot or icy, and I feel exhausted. The adrenaline is never released. It's like being forced to watch endless car collisions and air crashes. My nerves are slammed. I'm a wreck.

You've constantly got the hierarchy in your head; prisoners gnashing and scratching to clamber up and shove someone else down. The competition does your head in but I'm not cowed, and I could never give up and be an underdog like Daphne. But I hate what it turns me into—no better than a starving dog using any dirty fighting necessary to keep her place in the pack.

Leigh sauntered up to me and grabbed the roll-up out of my mouth and chucked it on the wet ground. "Oi, bitch, we've arranged a little surprise for your stroppy cellmate."

I froze. "Say that again." I turned to the great wall of tiny windows trying to make out Vee through ours. Fourth floor up, eighth from the left. I couldn't see any movement up there. I'd left the light on in our cell, and it looked like Vee was still huddled in her top bunk. I could just make out a bundle in the blankets.

"You are a sick bastard, Leigh. You know she's ill and not up to a booby trap today. I'm going to go up there–"

PEOPLE PERSON

But I was stopped by Leigh's beefy hand on my shoulder. "One more step and I'll make some nice tramlines on your face, know what I mean?" Low to my stomach I felt razor blades. I glanced down and saw she had pulled out a typical prison weapon: two blades melted into a snapped off toothbrush handle.

I knew exactly what she meant. I'd seen the mess those things had made of other women.

She had her arms round me, for all the world like she was giving me a friendly hug. All girls together. "What are you going to do to her?" I had to know. Aytrisha was near enough to wonder what was going on. She was looking over, and maybe if she overheard what Leigh was saying she could get up there to give Vee a chance. But Lorraine had arrived now, out of breath and grinning her wicked grin.

Lorraine twisted Aytrisha's arm up behind her back and marched her over to where Leigh had hold of me. "Oh, you've heard the good news!" Lorraine was crowing. "We've been waiting so patiently for a day when your dyke cellmate was spending the day in bed. Has she got lesbian clap from shagging you too hard?"

She was high, I could see that. Her eyes were completely blue; just tiny dots for pupils. She spat in my face and let the gob run down while Leigh held me. "Your little lesbie-friend is going to get a good *fucking*. That should make her a bit less up herself."

My stomach felt icy with fear. What were they going to do to Vee?

Everyone was outside milling about in the grounds. The screws would be oblivious in their common room, and Vee was alone and helpless. Like some sick pantomime we could suddenly see a huge dark shape stumble into her cell. With a wince, I said, "Alf. It's fucking Alf. You've set him loose in a vulnerable woman's cell." I couldn't say anymore because I was bent double by Leigh's trademark sledgehammer punch to the guts.

ALEX SPEAR

PEOPLE PERSON

Chapter Ten

Waiting tables in the evenings was exhausting, but it was better than washing up. A young girl who couldn't speak any languages any of us could recognize had arrived, so she was on bottle-washing duty, and I had been promoted to lowest waitress and skivvy. Being naturally inclined towards self-centeredness, remembering to give other people bread and jugs of water and booster seats was a struggle. I ran around, was hissed at by the staff above me in the pecking order (all of them) and learnt a lot about how to be practical. I also lost a ton of weight.

I was still living at Rachel's, although she had a live-in boyfriend now: Richard. They were *very much in love* but easy enough to live with. I hardly saw them anyway as I seemed to be needed at the restaurant from when they opened at lunchtime till hours after they'd closed.

I became a better friend as well. I paid my way around the house and let Rachel and Richard have their space. Travelling had made me realize that money is a finite commodity. I had never in my youth had to economize or choose between two things I wanted. Standing in a supermarket in Darwin, I had suddenly realized that I could either afford dinner that night or tampons, but not both. I had been spoilt before, and these tiny privations had been very good for me.

I didn't know what Virginie was going through in prison, but I hoped some of these challenges I had to deal with would make her see I was mature enough for a relationship with her. I thought it might bring us closer together once she knew we had these things in common.

Whenever I had a bit of spare money from a good night of tips it went towards clearing my Australia debt. Occasionally, I'd buy little bits of furniture as well: a nest of mini-tables or a cheap but sweet lampshade. In a half-assed kind of way, I wanted to make a little home for Virginie when she got out. I'd tried having a few other casual girlfriends but being with them made me feel lonelier. When I thought about the future, all I could see was Virginie. I prayed she felt the same way.

PEOPLE PERSON

Chapter Eleven

We saw a flurry of movement in the cell, and then, the light went off and we couldn't see any more. Leigh made me count out loud to a hundred before she let me go. "He'll have finished by now," Lorraine gloated, and I bolted back inside with Aytrisha. God knows what kind of state Vee would be in.

As we sprinted up the stairs Whitney was coming down.

I shouted to her through the netting between the banisters: "Have you seen Vee? Is she all right?"

Whitney snorted. "Yes, she's fine. Getting her kicks with the gardener."

"No, mate, you've got it all wrong. He went in to attack her."

Whitney said she had gone looking for Vee but had left well enough alone when she had caught sight of her in her pyjamas, standing in the middle of our cell trying to get Alf to have sex with her.

"She was wagging her crotch at him like this," Whitney did a prim little demonstration, her mouth pursed. "She looked desperate for it. She was saying, 'C'mon, big man. Show me what you've got. Show me what you can do'."

"Vee?" Aytrisha said, disbelieving. "She's not interested in any blokes, let alone Alf the Beast."

"All I'm saying is, if he is fucking her, she wanted him to," Whitney was adamant.

"I don't believe it," I said and ran up the stairs to our cell. I heard Aytrisha skidding along the corridor behind me.

Alf was standing in the doorway, his back to us. He was a great slab of a man, his broad shoulders somewhere up above my head, his thick muscles just about contained by his lumberjack shirt and jeans. He was blocking the way in, and I needed to get to Vee. "Alf," I shouted, sounding cockier than I felt. He turned to me, looking somewhere between angry and terrified.

I shoved my way through, and when he saw there were two of us he didn't argue. Vee was indeed standing in front of him, in her pyjamas, gyrating her hips like a lap dancer. Her face was virtually grey with exhaustion.

Alf shoved past Aytrisha and lumbered away down the corridor saying, "Sexy girl," to himself in his freaky, high-pitched voice.

Aytrisha was appalled. "Vee! What the hell are you doing, man? You wanted to, you know, with *Alf?*"

"No, of course I didn't," Vee snapped, leaning her full weight against the bunk. Her face was just running with sweat. "Help me get back into bed before I fall down."

As I helped ease her back under the covers, Vee explained, "I was just hoping he'd be the sort to get turned on by a helpless victim. I was hoping he'd freak out if a woman was sexually aggressive, and he would not be able to manage anything." She closed her eyes gratefully. "Thanks for coming up when you did," she said to us both. "He might have knocked me around a bit anyway, for appearances, and I'm not feeling at my most able to fight back."

"This was Lorraine and Leigh's doing," I told her. "This was their idea of revenge. You've got to watch your step with them, babe." I stroked her fringe back off her damp forehead. "Although, I've got to hand it to you, that was really smart thinking. Seems like you can deal with whatever shit gets thrown at you."

When it comes down to it, when you're a woman it's not about how big you are, it's about how clever you can be. Lorraine's a master at it, but I was learning that our Vee was too.

PEOPLE PERSON

Chapter Twelve

For once, it was me with a problem, but I wasn't sure whether I wanted to tell Vee about it. She was cross-legged on her bunk as usual, and I was lying on mine. We'd both had a bit of hooch, me a lot more than her, and it was that mellow time when the lights had just gone out, but you could get away with talking quietly before you fell asleep.

"Vee," I began. "Can I ask you something?"

"Yes, of course," she murmured through the dark.

"Do you ever get ... lonely?"

"... Huh?"

"What I mean is ..." Damn, this was hard. "Man, I'm drunk enough to just come out and say this to you. In the night, sometimes I'm virtually *howling* from the lack of sex."

"Oh, that. Yes, I know what you mean."

"Even my dreams let me down when I'm inside. I get this heavy, useless feeling that I'm just dragging my body around from place to place and it's never getting a workout, never being used for what it's meant for. I feel like heavy clay or playdough." I laughed at myself. "I catch sight of my breasts in the shower or my bottom in the mirror, and I want to shout out, 'Look! This is all going to waste!'"

"That's true. We're missing out on our youth."

"And I eat more ... complete rubbish, anything to be chewing, gnawing, burning up some of this frustration. I ... you know ... *touch myself,* probably everyone does ...."

"... Yep." Now, she laughed. It was a personal thing to admit. But the thought of it was making me feel a bit crazy. Maybe it was the hooch.

"But sometimes that's even worse, just doing it to yourself. It's not the same as being with someone else. It's not the same thing at all." I slapped the side of the bed and made all the little chains that held the mattress in dance above my head.

We were silent for a while. I hoped she hadn't gone to sleep. Eventually I said, "Vee ...."

A pause. "Yes ...."

"I'm not a lesbian. You know that ...."

After another moment, I heard through the darkness, "Yes, I know that ...."

This was awkward. "The thing is, I've always wondered ... what *exactly* it would be like ...."

I heard a noise. She had suddenly jumped down, and I could just make out her shape crouched by the foot of my bed. "You can't have a conversation like that with one of us virtually in another room," she whispered. "Now, what are you trying to say?" I could hear the smile in her voice. "Are you propositioning me?"

"Do you miss your ex?" I gabbled. "Do you get lonely in here?"

She thought about it. "It doesn't bother me too much to go without sex, I guess. I can hang on until I'm with the right person. Of course, it has been a while ...."

If I didn't say it now, I never would. "I'd really like to ..." I gulped. "I'd really like to know what it feels like to kiss a woman."

She kissed me, and it was nice. Her face was so soft, and her lips were hot and delicate, and obviously, there was no spiky stubble or big angular jaw going on.

"Now, you know," she whispered in my ear, and she clambered back up into her bunk.

PEOPLE PERSON

Chapter Thirteen

One of the screws, Jenny, isn't as bad as the rest. She seems like she does listen if you tell her something and will try and do something about it. The other screws all just want an easy life or else they're on a power trip. Anyway, Jenny took the trouble to come round to my and Vee's cell to pass on some bad news personally rather than let us hear it second-hand.

She quietly told us that Alf had managed to assault one of the women, and he would not be working here anymore. She apologized that he had been around as long as he had.

"Who did he get?" Vee wanted to know, furious.

"Whitney. She's in the san."

We went to see her as soon as we were allowed. She was lying on the small, white bed, looking more tiny and more defeated than ever. She had her legs pulled up to her chin and was hugging them to her so hard her fingernails were white. Any trace of fight she'd had in her was gone.

Vee tried to cheer her up and tell her she wasn't to blame. Whitney couldn't say much, but she squeaked out that it had brought back all the old memories of being abused as a child. She's always had men interfering with her. As soon as she ran away from home she became a prozzy. She didn't want to talk about what Alf had done to her, but the examination by the doctor afterwards seemed to have upset her even more. Whitney had tried to refuse, but the heartless nurse had been there and said she wasn't allowed to. "She said I had to have the ... internal exam, Vee," Whitney whispered, "so they could get his DNA. But when I asked her if that meant he would get taken to court about what he did, she said everyone would say I was asking for it anyway. So, why did they have to do that to me–?" She broke down completely, and Vee just gave her a hug and stroked her hair.

I was properly worried about Whitney. That's a bad look inside. You've got to look like you're strong. I've seen what happens to girls who lose their fight. What you've got to remember is most of the women in a prison have had terrible lives. They're full of anger and hurt, and they love nothing more than someone even lower than themselves to pick on.

Whitney came wobbling out of the san a few days later, and we helped her around a bit, but we couldn't watch her all the time. Lorraine cornered her in the dinner queue and started whispering to her. Whitney was looking miserable and nodding her head. I went over there in time to hear Whitney say, "But I'm off it now, Lorraine, so I don't want any for myself. I'll just hand it over to you straight away ...."

I'd heard enough. Lorraine's always on the lookout for a small, timid girl to use as a mule. She forces them to meet her fella or some other villain outside the prison on visiting day and bring the drugs in. The mule puts the drugs in the place the screws find it hardest to check, if you know what I mean. They *can* check there, of course, but it's a hassle for them, and quite often, you'll get away with it.

It's how Lorraine gets her smack, so she's dependent on a steady number of new mules. But don't think that means she's nice to them. She's like a monster where her drugs are concerned. One young girl clamped up down there from all the stress of bringing the stuff in, and she couldn't get it out, so Lorraine grabbed her and yanked her skirt up and just helped herself. The girl was in agony, but she hadn't dared make a sound.

PEOPLE PERSON

Chapter Fourteen

Lorraine came round to our cell and we were petrified, but she just seemed to want to shoot the breeze. Vee was sitting at the desk reading, and I was on my lower bunk tasting a tiny bag of hooch some of the women had managed to make. It tasted like mouldy vomit, but at least it was strong.

Vee had to pipe up, "Lorraine, I was disappointed you sent a man to dish out my punishment instead of doing it yourself."

"You shut your mouth," Lorraine said. "Don't get too big for your boots, dyke, or you'll be sorry."

"Can't you have a conversation?" Vee was relentless. "Do you ever think about why you do the things you do? We could all work together. If we use violence on each other, then the screws have won." Then she shut up because I had kicked the back of her legs as hard as I could.

Lorraine lowered her voice. "Whitney's doing a run at the next visiting morning, Saturday. Just make sure she does it and doesn't fuck up. Otherwise, I'll give all three of you something to smile about. You get me?"

I spoke loudly over Vee in case she was about to say anything else. "None of us want Whitney to get into trouble. We'll keep an eye on her."

When Lorraine had gone, I said to Vee, "Jesus, man!" But there was no telling her. That was the thing about Vee, she seemed like she had no fear of anyone. She just said what she thought. She didn't wind Lorraine up as a power trip, for example because she fancied running the place herself – she was just honest. It was scary, but she was getting a lot of respect from the women for it.

Vee did get a plot in the garden after she'd completed three years of her sentence. She worked hard on it, of course and immediately made the most amazing use of the small space. Everything she put in seemed to grow. She had small, square tufts of herbs, some vegetables, and cutting through it were small, bright flowers.

Vee knew how to make her plants into first aid for us all. If you had period pains or a headache or a cold, Vee would have some natural remedy for you. Half the time a woman was stressed or worried and just wanted someone to talk to, and Vee always seemed to have time. Most of us had ended up inside because we'd never had anyone show us a little patience, a little understanding, a little love even. We all looked for it among the wrong sort of men, villains and bastards, we knew that. But Vee didn't judge, and when you'd been through it all with her and cried yourself out, she'd have some common sense for you and you'd feel a bit better.

She did the job that bitch of a nurse and that work-shy Peterson should have been doing. At least Peterson ordered a few packets of seeds for her if she kept on at him long enough. Over the next couple of years, Vee was to be given another three plots, and she showed the women how to tend them, how to grow vegetables when they got out, to keep themselves and their families healthy.

Vee took to feeding herself from the garden as well, and she could be found sitting under a tree, nibbling a few salad leaves, a carrot, or a strawberry from her garden. I called her a rabbit, but she didn't care. She had started to look fresher and stronger with a bit more colour in her face. She seemed to be able to relax enough to eat when she was out there, and she looked younger too. She was only in her mid-twenties, after all, and had her whole life full of potential.

If a woman had man trouble or was fuming about an unfair punishment the screws had dished out, they'd go and find Vee, and they'd sit together under a tree and talk it out. Afterwards, Vee would stay there, looking at the sky until you thought she'd taken root. She

PEOPLE PERSON

once told me she felt like a plant, absorbing fear and pain and releasing it into the air.

Vee isn't wet like the counsellors and social workers though. I can't decide whether she's bloody brave or she's got a death-wish. I went to the prisoners' phone with Vee tonight, and Lorraine came up and seemed like she was queuing to use it too. Bloody Mason wasn't at home. He'd left the boys on their own again, and they told me they hadn't been to school all week. I was just replacing the receiver when I heard Vee saying, "... listen to you, if you ever want to talk."

Lorraine was looking horrified but had her head bent towards Vee, so it must have been her that Vee was talking to. Lorraine was just saying, "Well, I–" when she saw me and snapped her head up out of their huddle. "Why would I want to talk to you, dickhead," she shouted and barged in front of Vee to use the phone. I grabbed Vee and marched her away from the danger area.

ALEX SPEAR

PEOPLE PERSON

Chapter Fifteen

The last time I visited Virginie in prison, I had a surprise for her. "I've been working and saving up and being thrifty like you, and now ...."

"Yes, Felix?" She looked excited.

We were outside by the coach that brings all the visitors from the station. Other prisoners were greeting their families. I moved us away from a couple of young men who had such an edge to them that I hadn't even wanted to make eye contact on the coach, never mind speak to them.

"I'm debt-free. Those payments I had to make every month to pay back my Australia loan? All finished now. From now on, all my wages are for us." I broke off when I saw her face. "I thought you'd be pleased?"

"That's your big news?" She was scathing. "You've worked for five years to get back to square one? You spent a load of money you couldn't afford on *nothing*, and you've had to use all this time paying it back instead of saving for the future?"

"It wasn't *nothing*." She could be so cranky about money. "While I was travelling around, I was finding myself. You know, having an experience."

"Well, I've *found* myself in here for free," she said sarcastically.

It was true. She was a different person from when she'd gone in. She'd always been eerily competent, but now, she had the quiet self-confidence that comes from knowing you can cope with whatever happens. I realized with a horrible jolt that she didn't need me anymore. She would be fine wherever she went when she got out.

I wanted to go inside to the little area of plastic tables with her, but she said she just had to keep an eye on something for a minute.

"I've also been working and saving and going without luxuries," she continued, "and I'm just about to reach my goal—getting on for two thousand towards my deposit. With the four thousand I've still got in savings from grandfather when he died, I've got enough to put down a deposit on a little flat. If I can get a job when I'm free, that will pay the monthly mortgage repayments, and I'll be quite independent."

"What about us? I can support you quite well. You'll never have to lift a finger in my house, if you don't want to."

Those eyes. They flashed with danger. "How can I not *work*?" She was furious with me. "How can I not be *useful?*"

"I just thought we could live together quietly and contently ... put all this gritty prison stuff behind you."

"Maybe I don't want to be content," she said more to herself than to me. "Nothing to strive for, warm and sated and indolent, that would feel like suffocation."

Behind the rest of us, next to the coach, I thought I saw the little black girl with the terribly ill pallor pull up the front of her skirt, touch one of the scary men's hands, then touch herself, you know, *down there*. It was over in a second, and I was embarrassed to have even seen it. I supposed he was her boyfriend and it was some sex thing, but the scene bothered me. The girl looked so broken, like her spirit was gone.

I asked Virginie in a small voice, "Well, then. Can I come and see you sometimes?" It seemed like too much to hope that we would live together. "What I mean is, do you want to give things another try?"

At that moment, a toddler came tearing past us, and Virginie grabbed him and scooped him up. "Oops, can't have you going out there on your own," she said to him, kissing his head. The woman Virginie had pointed out as Daphne lumbered over with another toddler on her hip and said, "Oh, thanks, Vee," and retrieved the now screaming child.

PEOPLE PERSON

I didn't recognize my Virginie with her short hair and easy manner. When she came to eventually leave prison, it seemed she would be all sorted out and had a future mapped for herself. I had thought she needed me, but now my only chance was to make her *want* to be with me as a grown up, free woman. But Virginie seemed to be needed here among her new jailbird friends. They had even given her a new name. Would she ever be mine again?

We said goodbye. She gave me a little kiss, and I went outside. I couldn't bear to see her being led back to her cell. I went outside and was queuing to get back on the coach. Suddenly, the one called Lorraine was there, and she tapped me on the shoulder. She whispered that she had something to tell me. I left the line to follow her a short distance away.

"You know, your Vee isn't exactly keeping the home fires burning?" she mouthed, twisting one of her huge hoop earrings. "I'm only telling you 'cos it doesn't seem right for you to be waiting on the outside like an idiot and her carrying on the way she is."

"What do you mean?" I tried to push my way back towards the door to Virginie, but the prison guards were blocking the entrance now, and one of them came to round Lorraine up.

As she was led away she said, "Everyone knows about it and they laugh about you. She's at it with her cellmate, Twyla."

I didn't see a thing for the whole journey home. As soon as I had reception on my phone I called the prison number and asked to speak to Virginie. She was eventually allowed to come to the phone. I demanded to know whether she'd been unfaithful to me with her cellmate.

There was a silence. Then I heard Virginie's voice sounding uncharacteristically flustered. "I don't know how you heard about that. I never thought you'd find out. But being in here, I've got to be myself and get through it somehow."

She never thought to check what I was accusing her of. In her honest heart, a kiss was as bad as sex. And I was too enraged to check what she confessing to, so I assumed that Lorraine had been telling the truth and Virginie was having sex with Twyla. I hung up and turned my phone off, then shoved it to the bottom of my bag. How dare she? Enjoying nights of prison passion while I waited alone. Laughing about me with her new, rough friends. My former indiscretion was completely different, of course. I didn't deserve this. Well, that decided me. I wouldn't visit her again, and when she got out, she was on her own.

PEOPLE PERSON

Chapter Sixteen

"Before Lorraine gives birth we're going to have a proper mother-and-baby area," Vee announced one morning.

I looked up from my breakfast, a thin kind of home-brand porridge. "Who are you talking to, you nutter?" Sometimes she just said these mad things to herself. Vee was a funny one, but there was no harm in her.

But she was dead right about the mother-and-baby area. It was a horrible, shabby place; more a draughty old hall at one end of the prison with some splintery chairs and a peeling mural from the seventies. It was cold, it was unhygienic, and it was the only place that prisoners who were mothers with under-twos could let them run around. As soon as your kids reached the age of two they were supposed to stay with your family and manage without you on the outside. Also, when prisoners with young kids had their older kids visit them, the room could have been quite a nice place for them to all be together, except it was so rundown it made you feel even more depressed.

Vee asked to see the governor about it and was refused. She went round to find Peterson, the groundsman, and asked him if he had time to repaint the mother-and-baby area. I thought she'd complain about Alf, but she wasn't stupid. Saying anything just makes things worse.

We all knew that. Peterson said he had the paint but no time, and they wouldn't get onto it until at least next year. Vee asked if she could take the pots and do the painting herself, and Peterson said he couldn't care less if she drowned herself in it. So, Vee found the pots of paint in the sheds and dragged them inside, then asked the screws who ran the mother-and-baby area if she could give the place a paint and spruce up. The screws told her to fuck off and mind her own business. They also confiscated the paint. Vee asked again to see the governor about it needing doing and was refused again.

But things were changing. Women all over the prison had heard that someone wanted to sort out the baby area and they liked the idea. They could see the sense of it, and anything to do with kiddies was always a winner. But most importantly they got a definite sense that the screws and the governor were against it. Any ruse the establishment didn't like, we would move heaven and earth to make a success. Suddenly, women all over the prison were complaining about the lack of facilities for women with young kids. "That baby area is a disgrace. Why doesn't somebody do something about it? All the prisons I've been in had a better one than we've got." Vee got us stirred up when she told us she'd found out that any one of us could send a letter for free, and if we wrote a special number on the envelope the screws couldn't open it like they always did. We were all talking about it at meals and in the grounds. To wind the screws up, we deliberately announced in front of them that we were going to write to our families and get them to talk to the papers about the shit facilities for prisoners with kids.

The screws were getting edgy, you could see that. One night at dinner, it seemed like all you could hear round every table was loud conversations about it. We knew we'd succeeded in rattling them when they suddenly shouted that we were all to take our meals and finish them in our cells with the doors locked and no talking. Us old-timers knew what that meant, all right—they were expecting a riot. Good old Vee had put the fear of God into the screws just by speaking the plain truth.

The next day, Vee was summoned to the governor's office and was being told she *had* to paint the mother-and-baby area for no pay and no time off from her jobs in the laundry and the garden. We took this as a bizarre kind of victory as it was exactly what Vee had offered to do in the first place. A few of us divided up the work between us: me,

PEOPLE PERSON

Aytrisha, Fat Pat, and Lacy. And little Whitney said she'd help if we would show her what to do.

Vee got us to do it all properly. She didn't want us to cut corners. "If we make it nice and clean and wipeable in here, it will be safe for the kids," she said. We didn't have a paint stripper, so we were just going back over the old stuff, but Vee got us to wash it all down with sugar soap first. Then she wanted every rough edge sanded, sealed, or primed, and we seemed to take ages just preparing to start painting. Fat Pat complained, but Vee was tough. She knew just how she wanted it to be.

We painted the walls with a pale yellow she'd found in the shed, then she mixed up a lovely deep green for the skirting boards and round the windows. Vee wanted Whitney to design a new mural for one end. She knew Whitney could do it because Whitney was covered in tattoos in these beautiful, intricate designs that she'd come up with herself. Whitney was overjoyed to be asked and spent hours with her notebook and pencil. Finally, she decided what she wanted. I helped her draw it out much bigger on the far wall. It was an abstract set of shapes, a bit like the decorations on the plates at this Moroccan restaurant I used to go to on the outside. Whitney painted over it with the most intense shades of paint she could find from the little sample pots Vee had cadged out of the sheds. Whitney got out her precious makeup collection and mixed some of it with the paint, so she ended up with deep purple, hot pink, and turquoise, and she added some loose body glitter, so the whole thing sparkled. She picked out the details in an orange nail varnish. When she'd finished, it looked stunning.

Once we'd finished painting the room, Vee got us to take all the splintery chairs and tables outside. She'd found a load of sandpaper in one of the sheds, and she gave each of us a piece. She got us to sand, paint, and varnish each chair in bright colors. Finally, she bagged up all the rubber toys, teddy bears and tired old cushions and took them to the laundry to give them the cleaning of their life. All the colors came up beautifully, and the greyish film of dust that had settled on them over the years was gone.

Some of the women came down to admire our work. They were impressed. Daphne was chuffed that she'd have somewhere to take her youngest two when her mum brought them to visit her. "Thanks, Vee," Daphne said, and then we all started doing it, "Yeah, thanks, Vee."

But Lorraine strolled past, and she hates stuff going on that she's not in control of. "She's always bossing someone around, that dyke," was all she had to say about it. "What's the big drama?" She looked like she was about to do something horrible to the room, like the time she set fire to the prisoners' phone and seating area.

Vee burst out with, "I was trying to get it all sorted in time for you." She was exhausted from all the work on the room in addition to her long hours at the laundry.

"Me?" Lorraine said in a funny voice. Most people knew by now she was pregnant but hadn't dared say anything about it.

And to our amazement she left the room alone. Things are very odd around here.

PEOPLE PERSON

Chapter Seventeen

I don't think any of us were surprised when Whitney's body was found in her cell that weekend, hanged by her belt tied to her bunk. She was only light, so the belt hadn't broken when she'd jumped, which had saved other prisoners in the past. The nurse told us she would have been dead within seconds and probably hadn't felt much.

Vee felt guilty and responsible. "I should have known. I should have helped her more," she said. "Right before the end, she seemed more cheerful, really. I thought maybe she would get back on track—"

"That's quite normal," the nurse interrupted. She hadn't managed to look particularly upset about this death. She was a hard woman. "They often seem to cheer up once they've decided on a plan to kill themselves."

"But did you hear why she did it, Vee?" I said, closing the door as the nurse left. "Lorraine went berserk getting the stuff from her after she brought it in on visiting day. She really hurt her."

"I've heard that can happen," Vee said. "It's sick. But why would that make her …? I don't understand."

"Whitney had to go to the san afterwards, and it was so bad they sent her to the hospital for stitches. She hardly told anyone, but she found out she probably wouldn't be able to have children because of it.

That's what sent her over the edge. She's always wanted a family when she got her head straight."

"What the hell did Lorraine do to her?" Vee was shocked. But then, she's a first-timer. She doesn't know how evil the drugs make women.

"Like I said, Lorraine went berserk on her. She ... she didn't just use ... her fingers ...."

"What do you mean?"

"She used whatever she had at hand to get the drugs out of Whitney ... including a fork ...."

Vee looked like she was going to be sick.

After a while, she got angry. "They don't keep us safe in here. It's barbaric."

"You're telling me."

"Look at Whitney's last weeks on this earth! Raped by Alf and torn to pieces by Lorraine. We're like pieces of meat in here." She vowed to go on a hunger strike, and despite my knowing how those tend to be dealt with, I said she could count me in.

PEOPLE PERSON

Chapter Eighteen

Vee and I were held down, and I knew why. It was so the nurse could insert our feeding tubes. I watched Vee get hers. I tried to turn my head away, but the screw who held me wrenched my head round and said, "Just look. Look what you've done!" I saw what I'd done, all right.

Little Vee, her face already a mess of snot and blood, and the nurse pressing the tube into her nostril, feeding it through, not reacting to Vee's screams of pain. I've had it done to me before, so I knew that the tubes they use on prisoners are deliberately bigger than the slender ones they give hospital patients. The threat of being ruined by that big tube being shoved into your nose and down your throat is supposed to stop us hunger striking.

I watched the clock over her head from ten past to twenty-five past. It took the nurse fifteen minutes to get Vee's down, and her screams had become quiet whimpers, gulps, and shaky begging. "Please. Please stop," was all I could hear now and an occasional sucking noise of the tube breaching another section of Vee's soft insides.

The nurse came to me now, and the second before the fear made me blank out, I looked in her eyes and saw there was nothing there: no pity, no pain, no sign that she understood that she and I were human beings. Deep down, I'm always scared of hurting someone else because I've got this funny feeling that if it's OK to do it to someone else, it makes it OK for them to do it to me. But the nurse was like a machine.

She placed the end of the feeding tube to the soft membrane inside my nose and pushed. The pain began like the most maddening scratch, then built into a white-hot rip of agony. She breached my nose and her tube forced its way into the soft passage behind. I didn't cry. To cry you have to relax, and I was rigid. It took all my strength to concentrate on the burning in my face. I heard the sucking sound and felt the back of my throat shudder as she raped me. I heard a dry sort of sobbing and realized it was me. I was dizzy; bloodied mucus was drowning me. I snatched at breathing, but all I was aware of was the pain.

When she had got it in, the pain had lost its sharpness and became a terrible ache. The feeding came now: thin, white Complan down the tube and straight into the belly. You feel you're being overstretched by the liquid with no option to swallow or gag. You throw most of it back up anyway, so you hardly get any of the nourishment. It keeps you alive, barely—the governor can't have hunger strikers dying—and it also makes the point that they are in charge. Inside, you can't even choose not to eat; the most basic personal choices are taken away.

Vee suffered badly from this one. She had been so strong and sorted before, but this punishment looked like it could be the one to break her. Everyone's got a weak spot. I only prayed the screws wouldn't notice the change in her and use this particular torture on her whenever they got the chance. If you show fight and resistance, the screws get to know you as intimately as a lover, so they can use your individual self to control you and keep you down. For me, they know I'm a soft cow when it comes to my mates. That's why they made me watch Vee and told me it was my fault she was getting the feeding tube. That's the torture that breaks me and they know that.

PEOPLE PERSON

Chapter Nineteen

We were eventually allowed to leave the san after the feeding tubes had been carelessly ripped out of us. I was resting on my bed, broken. I could barely perceive the conversation Vee was now holding from her bunk. The words didn't register in my mind as I held my destroyed face and tried not to be consumed by my misery.

I could hear Lorraine saying to Vee, "You remind me of a teacher I had in secondary school. She was bossy like you, but people didn't mind. And she was always saying stuff like, 'You don't care who you …'" she paused and made a noise of frustration, "Whatever it was you said."

Vee then asked a question that made me suck in my breath.

"Lorraine, you seem a bit upset today? Is anything the matter?"

"Fuck off!" Lorraine suddenly shouted, and without warning she punched Vee round the head. "You fuck off as well, pikey!" she shouted at me and ran out of our cell and slammed the door. It sounded like a car crash.

Much later, she came back. "Can I talk to you?" Lorraine muttered to Vee.

"I don't know. My ears are still ringing," Vee said sarcastically. She's not scared of anyone; you've got to give her that.

Lorraine bashed me out of the way, so she could shut our cell door. What was she going to do to the pair of us now?

Vee was cross-legged on her top bunk, eyes glittering.

"It's just that some of the stuff you say about thinking and working out why you do what you do …" Lorraine looked appalled by what was coming out of her mouth. She carried on talking like she had no control over it. "Thing is, the whole thing with Alf sounds really stupid, but when I'm inside, I feel like … a little kid again. *I will kill you if you repeat this to anyone.*" She glared at us both and I didn't doubt it for a second.

"We'll keep it to ourselves. You know that," Vee said kindly. "Go on."

"I mean, when I'm banged up I feel, well, trapped, obviously, but it's more than that. I get proper nightmares. It's like all those stupid fears you have when you're a kid—ghosts, demons, witches, fucking vampire bats—they're all back again. Nothing's off limits." She kind of laughed at herself, but it was a scary sort of laugh, and I wondered whether she was high. "I have to jump into bed in case a hand shoots out from under it and grabs my ankles."

"I know what you mean," I said, grinning at how pathetic we both were. "Being locked up in the dark plays tricks on your mind. We're all kids again."

Vee was looking intense, the way she does when she's figuring something out; she becomes all eyes. "Didn't you feel safe in bed as a child, Lorraine?"

Lorraine's face went dark. "I'm not getting into that. I had a fucking stupid counsellor who only made it all worse. That's when the nightmares started. Anyway, he's dead now, the cunt."

"Who?" Vee looked like a statue.

"My fucking, lying, disgusting dad." Lorraine gave the most enormous kind of hiss, like there was a lot of pressure to be released.

"He abused you?" Vee asked.

"Oh, God," I said. I didn't know what to say. Her own father? Jesus.

"He used to play mind games," Lorraine went on, her face a funny, smiling, leering picture of rage. 'Let me do this to you and I won't do it to your little sister. Tell your mum about this and I'll have to slit her throat.'" She swallowed hard. "I left home as soon as I could. Moved in with my 'boyfriend,' who was almost as bad. He was forty and I

PEOPLE PERSON

was fifteen. I didn't stand a fucking chance. I look back on myself at that age and I think, 'That wasn't *fair*.' I should have had time to be young. Men should have left me in peace. I was a child." She punched the wall, then cradled her fist in pain.

"That's right," said Vee quietly. "It wasn't fair. You've got every right to be angry."

"Well, anyway," said Lorraine, angrily wiping tears away, "I'm not a victim anymore. I control this place."

"You don't control a thing."

"Whoa, Vee!" I jumped in. "That's harsh!"

"It's the truth," Vee said, calmly. "There's a man on the outside getting rich off your addiction, Lorraine. So long as you're an addict, you have no choice over anything you do."

People always seemed to learn from Vee, even if they initially thought she was talking rubbish. In this case, I don't think Lorraine had ever felt so understood.

Lorraine gave birth to a little girl in the nearby hospital with a police guard and was driven straight back to the prison as soon as her baby was pronounced strong enough to survive the journey. Lorraine wasn't checked out for her strength and lay in the san trying to breastfeed, crying out at the pain of her stitches down below. The nurse was unsympathetic, as you can imagine.

But Lorraine was able to use the bright, cheery mother-and-baby area. She grudgingly accepted some more counselling, and although she was always saying loudly to Leigh that it was all bollocks, she said she didn't want to be an angry mum and she ought to get her head straightened out for her daughter.

Vee served seven and a half years of her fifteen-year sentence and walked free on a beautiful, autumn day, all golden light and brown leaves. Some of the girls had promised to keep her vegetable gardens going. "You keep your nose clean, Vee. I don't want to see you back here again," I told her, giving her a bear hug by the main gates.

"You won't see me back," Vee promised. "I'm not going to wait another day for my life to begin." At the age of thirty, she was free.

ALEX SPEAR

PEOPLE PERSON

PART THREE

When the way comes to an end, then change - having changed, you pass through.

I Ching

Character is destiny.

Anon

ALEX SPEAR

PEOPLE PERSON

Chapter One

Outside the prison gates, Mason stood languidly by the bus stop. He lounged. He had visited his partner, Twyla, to pass on some drugs for her to distribute as usual. He was fairly safe because he had two of the prison officers working for him, shielding him from detection and allowing him to carry out his business of supplying the prison with the lower level drugs. He had also briefly visited Twyla as he needed a signature from her to sign the child benefit over to him.

Mason clocked the girl waiting by the bus stop, looking adorably fragile and vulnerable. Cropped, shiny, messy hair, and slender and self-effacing. She had clearly just been released. She had some sort of bin liner over her shoulder with a mass of perhaps clothing inside. He noticed her slim legs straight away, in the prison-issue grey tracksuit bottoms he was used to seeing Twyla in. The girl made a nervous movement, her head to the side, one foot pointed to the ground and tracing a small circle. Mentally he compared and rated their asses. This bint was tighter and more shaggable. She clearly hadn't had kids. A slightly shy cow, hopefully with an innocence he could exploit. When they had just been released, they were often alone in the world, he knew.

As Mason sauntered closer to her, he had no specific plan, but he caught her eye and didn't let it drop. She met his gaze and to his slight irritation, she did not look shy or remotely intimidated by him. She seemed world-weary; cautious but not scared of anyone.

"On your way into town?" he started. She nodded. He stared at her perky chest, visible beneath the tight grey material of her zip up hoodie. "What's your name, sweetheart?"

"Well, it's Vee, or Gina," mumbled the girl, flushing a little. Her new name for her fresh start. She looked annoyed at the question and perhaps regretted answering it honestly. She was slightly perplexed, he could see that in her face. He liked knowing he had made her uncomfortable.

"You got somewhere to stay tonight, Gina?"

She froze now. The bus was approaching. She walked towards the bus stop, away from him, not looking at him.

"Oi, I said, you got somewhere to go?" He walked after her and was just about to reach out and make her turn, when the bus pulled up alongside them both.

She hopped on and used the borrowed money to pay her fare. Mason didn't pay, and the bus driver knew better than to mention it. Mason followed the girl down the length of the empty bus and when she sat down at the very back, he stood near her in the aisle, one hand on each seat back on either side, barring her way out.

"I know you've just been let out, Gina. I know it's hard." He kept up this fairly loud monologue, embarrassing her and wearing her down. "I know they put you out without a penny to your name, and if you've got no one to meet you, no one who's been paying your rent while you've been inside, it's like you've dropped off a cliff. And then, you've got to start again but you've got nothing. I could help you. Look at me. Look at me, Gina."

She stared out the window, her face red, pretending she couldn't hear him. The hour and a half bus journey through the country lanes back to Swinton seemed to take at least twice as long under his badgering. She wished she could have afforded the train, but even if she had had the money, there was no coach to take them to the station that day. When at last they reached her stop, she had to face him. It was mid-afternoon and a weekday, and no one else had got on the bus, so they were still alone. She raised her eyes and said, "I'm getting off now. Please excuse me."

He walked slowly backwards the length of the aisle and jumped off the bus with her, never taking his eyes off her, relishing the opportunity

PEOPLE PERSON

to box her in and dictate the speed she could walk. As the bus pulled away, Mason insisted on taking her phone number. With a fluttering heart and tears in her eyes, she wondered whether she could refuse, or give him a false number. Unfortunately, he could apparently read her motives on her face, perhaps because she was unaccustomed to lying.

"I'll just phone it as soon as you tell me, Gina, and make sure you haven't given me the wrong number,"

She told him, finally defeated. He always had that effect.

"Hold up! I'm going to call you!" he said, gripping her shoulder as she tried to walk away.

"I haven't got any credit, and it's not charged up!" she squeaked, starting to really cry now. "Please let me go and leave me alone." She was pleading.

Mason gave her a look of wounded innocence. "I'm just trying to help ya, Gina! I see a young gel on the bus by herself, just been let out, and I try to make sure she's all right. Cor, you can't say anything these days."

With a grin, he watched her run away. He admired that little ass as she scuttled. He noted the address she ran to and typed the details into his phone to join the contact number she had had to give him. He saved it under the name 'Gina Jailbird.'

ALEX SPEAR

PEOPLE PERSON

Chapter Two

The children of Swinton creep to the murder house on their way home from school. They dare each other to peep in at the windows, even to go inside, but they run away screaming with delighted terror before nightfall. They've heard the rumour about the ghost that bangs and crashes around in there all night long.

It's a terraced house, just like all the others in that row. The murder house looks rather shabby as it has stood empty and unloved for such a long time. It had been bought by a property developer, who was then clearly in no hurry to get it cleared and back on the market. One of the upper windows is broken, but through the broken shards a thick iron mesh that has been used to board all the windows is clearly visible, and the front door has an enormous steel plate screwed over it. But the local children have found that this steel plate is affixed on one side to crumbling bricks, and they have managed to remove enough bricks to create a gap just barely big enough to crawl in.

This vandalism can't be seen from the road due to the huge skip the property developer hired and left in front of the house for months, which was gradually becoming filled with other people's rubbish. The area is too restrained and the children too innocent for much graffiti to have appeared. Swinton is educated working-class mostly, with white vans but no burnt out cars. Virginie's former front garden is full of weeds, creating a sort of canopy which holds aloft a riot of litter: cans, bags, and newspapers.

Just as the moon disappears behind a cloud, the ghostly noises begin. A thump from the back of the house and then a long pause. The children strain their ears. They are delighted by the terrifying sound of something heavy being dragged along the old floorboards. Then rummaging and rummaging like the devil going through his winter wardrobe. The children scream and run away.

It's Virginie, of course. Calls herself Gina now. The police suggested that she go by a different name as she is out of prison. "Put it all behind you," they said, "eradicate the association in other people's minds." She lives in a tiny box room in Tracy's house, that's Tracy of the front-room-turned-veggie-restaurant. Tracy needs the extra pair of hands at Gaia Veg Café enough not to judge, and she remembered the sweet young girl Virginie had been before all her trouble with the law. And at night, Gina goes back to the scene of her childhood.

The house had been left exactly as it was. Still piled high with all the possessions her mother and grandfather spent their lives amassing. Gina is slender enough to crawl through the children's loose part of the boarding, but she found her own insecure section of the security netting round the back door, which she can prise off and slide through. She seems to stay up all night now, sorting through the familiar, horrible things with a relentless fury.

Her time in prison had never been a fitting punishment. Now that she was out, her penance would begin; piecing together the life that had been lost. Really getting to know the woman that had been murdered.

Books and more books—old books, some with flaking brown pages and some with frayed cloth covers—and vinyl records and cassettes. Then clothes and more clothes—mad clothes that would never be worn, grubby aprons, miniskirts in enormous sizes, T-shirts for bands that had long since gone out of fashion, jeans with broken zips, shoes with flapping soles and broken-down backs, seventies' clothes, eighties' clothes, nineties' clothes, warm coats with the stuffing falling out, light-colored jackets spotted with grease, and cardigans with all the buttons cut off.

But before long, she started to unearth earlier layers. She cleared back the generic items and began to reach far more personal items—loose photos. They were not safely stored, just piled on top of the final layer, which consisted of diaries.

PEOPLE PERSON

Diaries?

And then she pulled out the diaries ... years and years' worth. They dated back to the Medusa's childhood. Gina forced herself to find all of them before she opened the first one. She piled them up on the table in date order and scoured the books and clothes until she had almost a complete set.

Gina sat down to read the diaries, beginning with the earliest one she could find. She had forgotten her mother's real name had been Mathilde. Grandfather had apparently had a penchant for slightly pretentious French names, perhaps inspired by his own, Victor. Medusa had evidently kept up the tradition when naming her own children, Virginie and Hugo, but her diary was not one of a dutiful daughter or even a happy daughter. Gina was shocked to read how miserable Medusa had been in 1953 at the age of thirteen.

She read: *"1st January. Father won't let me out again. The Baker sisters and Tommy and Susan were all going to the big field to play in the snow but father said I wasn't to go. Just seeing my friends at school isn't enough. We're always having to do work and be quiet. I just want to run around and shout and laugh and dance."*

"2nd January. Father said it was my fault the flour in the pantry went mouldy, and he's keeping me in through the holiday cleaning it all out. He said if I hadn't been such a slattern and had cleaned the pantry properly to start with, the flour wouldn't have spoiled. I can't wait till I am a woman with my own house. I will leave everything any old how, and I will have as many things as I like. I will never clean anything or tidy up or put anything away. I will live like an animal or a bird; wild and free. He won't even be allowed in my house."

Gina tried to remember whether she'd ever been told when and why her grandfather had come to live with them. Medusa had never said anything, but Gina could remember Miss Long, her primary school teacher, asking her whether it was fun having her grandfather stay with them all the time. Gina had never really wondered how Miss Long had known about it. Medusa knew teachers and people like that because of her job, so Gina supposed that was how. Back then, Medusa had seemed omnipotent, and the young Virginie had not questioned the network of power that surrounded her, keeping Virginie held as tight as if she had creepers round her neck.

When Medusa reached the age of eighteen, the diaries became battered notebooks rather than proper diaries. The next few seemed to have been bought abroad if the text and price labels on the covers were anything to go by. If Gina had to guess, she would say that one looked Spanish, one Turkish, and one Russian.

The story contained in the diaries was one of rebellion and hard-won freedom. When Medusa had been Mathilde, the wild girl with the incredibly lithe, muscular figure that was so admired and envied, she had run away from her controlling father and found herself dancing across Europe to the tune of the sixties. She made love, she tried drugs, and she hitchhiked everywhere with no belongings but a spare cotton dress and a bottle opener in her battered, cloth knapsack. She lived on her wits and her charm. She was a hit with men and women wherever she went.

She had come home again, earlier than she had ever expected, pregnant with Virginie. It seemed from the tone of the diaries that she had given her daughter that name to curry favour with her tyrannical grandfather. For young Mathilde, the free spirit, was now the shame of Swinton: an unmarried mother, a silly girl who had gotten herself into trouble with no money and nowhere to go. She moved in with an abusive older boyfriend in the grimy end of town and sent Virginie to live with her grandparents. By the time Mathilde escaped from the boyfriend, she was pregnant again. She named her little boy Hugo in a desperate attempt to link him to his grandfather and crawled home. The freest of girls had become the most trapped.

Mathilde's mother had looked after the children for a few years around that time while Mathilde had gone out to work. She had no qualifications or experience and was rejected everywhere she applied, but finally clawed and charmed her way into a cleaning and tea-making job at the council offices. The next few years' diaries consisted of scant entries, clearly reflecting what a busy life the young woman now led. One entry dated October 21st read:

"Virginie and Hugo woke each other up all night, crying from midnight till dawn. Had to be at work for half seven to clean the council chamber. Didn't get away till gone six. Cooked liver and onions for our dinner. Fell asleep in sitting room listening to radio with mother."

Despite the exhausting life of a working, single mum, over the years of Mathilde's diaries it became clear that she had caught the eye of several council members who liked having a cheeky, attractive girl around. By 1976, when her two children were at primary school, it

PEOPLE PERSON

seemed that Mathilde made full use of her assets to fight her way into secretarial duties, much to the consternation of the other secretaries who had had to complete typing and shorthand courses to get their jobs. By the time her own mother died, Mathilde was enjoying a reasonable standard of living for a mother of two without a husband, though she had to compete hard for her salary, and she was attending council meetings as a novelty, indulged by the patronizing old men in suits. The men on the council loved the saucy girl in her tight cardigans and pencil skirts berating them on their lack of provision in the town for mothers and children.

The more her father tried to control her and prevent her from having the career she was financially dependent on and the life he was so envious of, the more formidable Mathilde became. The rows she described in her diary were of the most explosive, emotional kind.

In 1978, Mathilde had moved out and rented this very terraced house with the two children. Gina suddenly put the diary down for a moment and tried to remember their house when they had first moved in. She thought she could see, in her mind's eye, the carpets clear and the corridors not stacked high with possessions.

But Mathilde must have found her freedom too loose, too empty, and she had begun to amass the clutter that would surround her for the rest of her life, calming her with its reverberations of her mental confinement.

Was it because Mathilde had spent so many years trapped and berated by a cold man that she had been easy prey for Reginald Pathaway? Despite her valiant fighting against the bars of her father's control, the patterns they formed had still been absorbed by her idealistic mind. She had accepted Pathway's authority because he felt familiar; there was a safety and a comfort in the old restraints.

Gina found that one diary entry swam before her every time she read it because her eyes had filled with tears. "I feel ugly in his house ... ugly and powerless." That was *exactly* how Virginie had felt when she had been living in her mother's house as a child, though she had never articulated it.

The restraints of her mother's childhood, both physical and psychological, had become her own in a terrible cycle of abuse. It was all so clear to see now.

ALEX SPEAR

PEOPLE PERSON

Chapter Three

And what was I doing now that Gina was out of prison and living in Swinton?

Well, my life hadn't stood still while she'd been inside, and I was still the same old Felix: lazy, unreliable, and able to make people feel like they're at a party. I had found, to my horror, that the irritating need you have in your twenties to have a job, translated by your thirties into a nightmarish need to have a *career*. What kind of a rubbish set-up is that?

Anyway, I'm afraid I just can't be competitive. I must be a human being. I make mistakes. I forget to do things I've said I'll do, mostly because I've said I'll do it just because I thought I should, and it was a boring thing I couldn't be bothered to remember. I let people down. But how ever annoyed they get with me, they always like to have me around; they say I'm the life and soul of the party. So, these days, I organize events. I can't think of a better job than planning kick-ass parties.

It just came about by accident while I was working at the restaurant. Whenever there was a special event or birthday party, I would always make suggestions. For example, having a load of balloon animals, or champagne cocktails fizzing with edible glitter, or hiring in a face painter or a fortune teller, and the punters went wild for it. Pretty soon, I was taken off my short order duties, so I could plan the events full-time. Eventually, I got poached by a promoter, and now, I work with pubs and clubs. Finally, I'm getting paid for the life I always lived anyway: sleep all day and party all night.

A party is basically bringing people together, and if you do it right those people will remember they had an amazing time, but they won't realize they didn't make it happen themselves. It can be hard to get the credit but, after a few of my events, regular attendees will say, "I like Felix's bashes; they always go off with a bang."

The whole Charmaine thing was long over. I still see her around Swinton. The funny thing was, even when we were going out together, whenever I saw her I was always disappointed. Thinking about her before a date in my imagination, she had seemed to be sexual perfection, a fantasy woman. The scenarios I played through in my head were always incredibly explosive sex where nothing boring or inconvenient ever happened. When I saw her in the flesh (and there was plenty of that) I would suddenly be confronted with how ordinary she looked. Her solid, sturdy frame was not quite the voluptuous vision I had been expecting. Her face was plain, and the width of her nose and the slight gap between her two front teeth made her look almost a little stupid.

Virginie never disappointed me. She wasn't ready to go out with me again, but she hadn't said that would never happen. I was still stinging from her betrayal and was too proud to talk to her about it. She had met me for a coffee twice since she had got out, and she had told me all about her house-clearing project, mostly because she had no one else to tell, I think.

As soon as I saw her, I was always lit from the inside, filled with a steady happiness and a joy that didn't need my imagination to make it seem more than it was. I was furious with her for being unfaithful to me, but I still loved her company, and the older I got, the more precious I realized that was.

I remembered the last few months of going out with Charmaine. Our conversation had become so stilted, and I've normally always got something to say for myself, but we had so little in common and our conversations had usually stuttered into an awkward silence. In the early days, I had filled these with a lingering kiss and probably a grope of those mammoth bosoms. But the excitement had long since died

PEOPLE PERSON

away, and kissing her had seemed scarily intimate, as if I would have to get to know her better if I continued to be so physically close, and I didn't want to do that.

Parties are what I do best. Keep it light and fun and don't think too much. I had arranged an event of my own that night, and I prayed that my guest of honour would turn up.

ALEX SPEAR

PEOPLE PERSON

Chapter Four

I was late as usual, having been up all night and then sleeping till teatime and through the alarm I had set to go off at 5pm. Gina was already in the café where we'd arranged to meet, her brows low.

"You're late, Felix! I've been here half an hour!" she exploded at me.

I grabbed her in a big hug and she softened. "Sorry. I'll make it up to you. Have we got time for me to have one of those?" I looked longingly at her empty coffee cup. I had a hangover and a slight cold, as ever.

"Not if the table's booked for seven. It serves you right," she grinned. "Come on." And she dragged me out of the café.

I was grinning from the hug. "I did try to call you. You need to keep your mobile switched on." Being close to her felt like a win on the lottery. She smelt of vanilla. "I know you think it costs money to have it switched on, but you're thinking back to pre-prison, my little jailbird." She wore a knee-length dress, and I couldn't take my eyes off those calves.

We were going to Chariot; my choice. Now I worked there, I was entitled to a miserly staff discount, and she finally felt enough at ease with herself to relax in a posh place. It was still getting brilliant reviews for the food, so I wanted to share it with her. The thought of giving her sensual pleasure of any type was enough to make me save up and put on a clean shirt.

When we'd been seated by my mate, Nico, and Gina'd refused any bread, we were alone in the candlelight. Staff could only book a table when it wasn't busy, and so we were early enough that there were no other diners at the tables near ours. I asked her how her house-clearing was going.

"I found another of Mummy's diaries, one of the missing ones." Her eyes lit up with the passion she had for her project. "Mummy described an argument she had with me. I must have been about thirteen, and I can remember it as well. Can you imagine getting to hear the other person's thoughts on an argument you had with them?"

"Wow, that must be weird." I couldn't really imagine my mother being dead, but I tried my best to understand what Gina was going through. "What was the argument about?"

"It was when the Patels first moved in. I remember trying to keep my temper while she was ranting on. She was always so angry about new people moving into our road. In her diary she makes herself sound quite reasonable, but what I remember is her just shouting, 'They could be anyone! Could be anyone!'"

It was quite disturbing how much like her mother Gina looked when she imitated her.

"She said, 'At least when Rebecca and Robert Price arrived, we realized they had known Elizabeth on the corner, so she could vouch for them. This new couple who've bought 42, nobody even knows their *name*. They could be anybody. It's like when those council houses down the end got bought under the right to buy. Now, absolutely anybody could move in.'"

Gina looked so sad and wistful I wanted to gather her up. "Mummy carried on ranting no matter what I said, but it was more to herself, and her voice was less strong, more … *frightened*, like an old woman. She just kept saying, 'Could be anybody!' I was so angry with her. She said she was going to get her busybody friend (Reginald, of course) to find out who they were. She made all these excuses about why it was important to vet people who moved in. She was obsessed by thieves and squatters – she feared the unknown. I'm not sure she cared that the Patels were Asian, that was more Reginald who was racist. Her big problem was that no one knew them."

PEOPLE PERSON

She lowered her head slightly and blew out her breath. Talking about her childhood always seemed to take it out of her.

"I can remember just trying to make her understand, saying, 'Mummy, for all we know they might be very nice! And we don't own the street! Anyone can buy a house!' But I was so busy being angry with her for her bigoted, small-minded objections, I never listened to what she was actually worried about. She was so scared of people. She got overwhelmed by anything new." Gina gave a huge sigh. "Poor Mummy. I didn't really want to upset her, but I just couldn't calmly listen to her version of life. It sounded so wrong, so paranoid and negative. Life to me seemed so different, and I wanted to share it with her. When I got away from all her cluttered thoughts, what I saw were possibilities and excitement, and new people were the best."

"What did her diary say, then?"

Gina looked so ashamed, it was heartbreaking. "From her point of view, she just wanted some comforting, for her daughter to agree with her. It confused her that we never seemed to understand each other. She had spent her whole life being told she was wrong and wicked. She just wanted a little praise for being right. Why couldn't I ever give her that?"

Our starters arrived: chilled pea soup for Gina, scallops and bacon for me. Gina had a funny way of looking small; kicking her legs on the slightly high, wooden chair, waiting obediently as Nico flung the crisp napkin over her lap, then set the huge white plate in front of her on which the tiny cup of soup was balanced.

I had to cheer her up. "You've got to remember how irrational she was, though. I remember that time I was sat in your kitchen and she was getting a bee in her bonnet about the bus service to that nearby village. Don't you remember?"

She wrinkled her forehead. "No? What happened?"

"You must remember. She had brought Gladys and George from ... Oh, what was it called? Started with a B."

"Betherbourne!"

"You do remember!" I almost cheered. Several nearby diners turned to stare snootily at us.

She lowered her voice. "Yes, Gladys and George. I haven't thought about them in *years*. Only a few people live in Betherbourne, and Mummy was adamant they needed a more frequent bus service."

"I can remember the whole conversation," I cut in. I didn't want Gina to look through her guilt-tinged memory and see her mother as anything other than crazy and harmful. "Gladys started by telling your mother that they had always had a very good, local shop. Then she said that when the wholesalers moved, the village shop went out of business, and she and George couldn't manage get all the way into Chipping any more.

"George reminded her that the milkman did bread and eggs. Gladys said, 'Yes, but for meat and veg it was either a case of waiting for someone to give them a lift or it was a two-mile walk to the convenience store with no pavement ....'"

"... and two arthritic hips!" Gina and I finished together. "I do remember her saying that! I'm so glad you were there. It was hard to go through these mad things by myself."

I wasn't going to be put off. "Then you said, what about a delivery from the supermarket. You have to spend a certain amount, but maybe there was a way of clubbing together with neighbours to order the bits needed, and split the cost. Gladys and George said they had wondered about doing something like that before but hadn't known who to pal up with. It would have been perfect."

Gina had been trying to eat her soup, but this conversation wasn't helping. She had managed a bite but had been circling the bowl with her spoon for the last five minutes. I had eaten one of my scallops but was too animated at this moment to enjoy them. I set my fork down for the denouement.

"Your mum just bellowed over us all, 'Outrageous! Older people in our community should not be forced into all this endless change. I will write again to Turner's about the bus times.' Then Gladys tried to say to your mum that they had thought about how many old folks there were in the area who could do with a delivery of food, and if they all went in together they would be spending enough to make it worthwhile. All they needed was someone to organize it and maybe distribute the food to the different households that needed it. And then *you* said–"

"I said, 'Mummy, you could do that,'" Gina whispered.

"And that was when she really flipped. She was *mental*. She was saying, 'Why are we making older people learn about all these difficult new things? Why are we forcing them into the modern world? Life used to be simple. They've lived through war and rationing, so why

PEOPLE PERSON

aren't we looking after them? Why must we have this endless complication dressed up as progress?"

Gina said, "I do remember. She jabbed her finger at me while we all just sat there in silence. She said, 'What Gladys and George need is a proper bus service, and that is what I am going to get them. I *will* make Turner's see reason. They *must* lay on buses every day, throughout the day, despite their silly objections about profits. The customer used to be right.' No one had dared say another word, like always. I was full of guilt that she had got so agitated because I knew it would take her hours to calm down and she'd be exhausted and fearful afterwards."

Gina visibly steeled herself and ate a spoonful of soup with an air of grim determination. "What I didn't work out at the time was that it was *Mummy* who felt left behind by progress and was longing for a return to a simple way of life. That confusion and loneliness comes through in her diaries."

"She never seemed confused," I said, spearing a scallop.

Gina shook her head. "I wouldn't have wanted a quiet, dutiful mother at home with a pinny on. I'm proud of having a mother people knew and respected. It was just that, well, now, I sort of know a bit more about her, and I realize she was trying to reject the kind of control or dominance that she had had to put up with from Grandfather. She had to reject it to such an extent that she insisted on being in charge wherever she went and in every sphere she heard about. It made her extremely effective as a campaigner. She was a formidable political opponent. But to be one of her children was quite terrifying."

"You mustn't blame yourself for what you … did in the end. She could have done a huge amount of damage, and she wasn't happy. You did her a favour with that condition she had."

"I don't know how much that condition had to do with her moods and her paranoia. I think she had more mental health problems than anyone realized. She could have had it for years and none of us knew. She never would go to the doctor; couldn't bear someone else telling her what to do even if it was for the good of her health. All I really wanted was a little moderation in her fierce disposition. She was dealing with me and Hugo, and we were *children*. She didn't seem to know that young minds need gentle handling. And it would have been wonderful if we could have had a little more comfort and order within our childhood home. I knew how to create it, or rather, I could spot all the things Mummy did that prevented it. But she had almost a *phobia* of being dictated to, of being externally controlled, even so far as listening to a sensible suggestion. She would fight against it with all her adult experience and never sheath her grown-up vocabulary and force of communication, even when she was dealing with me, her daughter, from such a young age."

Nico came to clear away our plates. He raised his eyebrows when he saw that both were still half full of food. "Have you finished?" he checked.

"Yeah," I muttered, pushing my plate away slightly. The scallops had gone cold, and the bacon tasted greasy now. Gina had managed precisely two spoonfuls of her soup.

When he had gone, Gina said, "The one thing I've never understood is why Mummy fell for Reginald Pathaway's manipulation. He always dictates to everyone he meets, particularly women. He seems to assume he is in control of all females."

"Felt comfortable, I suppose. From what you've said, your granddad used to be like that before he got old and doo-lally."

"Yes, I think that was it. I had wondered if it was something like that."

My steak arrived. My stomach growled at the scent of creamy peppercorn sauce and the sight of the matchstick fries piled up. Gina had opted for a simple dish of stir-fried greens and rice. She optimistically dug her fork into the steaming pile and fed herself a large mouthful. "Delicious," she said, experimentally, as if trying out a new language.

I walked her back to Tracy's. I couldn't bear to even try for a goodnight kiss. The thought of her betraying me with some prison piece broke my heart every time I remembered it. She looked pretty sad but didn't touch me at all on the walk home and just said, "Good night, Felix. I had a lovely evening. Thank you," then virtually ran inside.

PEOPLE PERSON

Chapter Five

Virginie cleared her throat and made a nervous gesture, her head to the side, the toes of one foot pointed and tracing a wiggle on the polished wooden floor. She fumbled with the cards on which she had printed her speech.

Miss Long had never married but she had become the headteacher of Virginie's former school. Her still pretty face was lined and tired but burst into a grin as her troubled former pupil addressed the current children who were cross-legged on the floor.

"I would like to tell you today a bit about the rehabilitation of people who have been in prison, like me," Virginie stammered to her solemn audience. "Some people think I shouldn't be honest about my experience. Some people think I should pretend I didn't go to prison. But my favourite teacher, Miss Long, always used to advise me: 'Tell the truth even when it is hard.'"

The children were wide-eyed as Virginie gently explained some of the nicer parts of her story. The friendships she had made inside. The progress with the mother and baby room, which had been expanded into a decent-sized centre thanks to her continued campaigning now she was free. The volunteering she still did to advocate for the women. The program she had insisted on for prisoners who were addicted to drugs, and for those at risk of suicide. She had breathed new life into initiatives that had been run in a tired and under-funded way.

One of the little boys put his hand up to ask her a question. "Did it feel scary to be locked up?" he breathed. The other children looked on in wonder.

Virginie thought for a moment, tempering her response. "I hope none of you ever do end up in a similar situation, but I think it wasn't that bad because I just waited." She considered this and then, smiled. "Yes. I just waited. It might be hard to wait, but you can do it. Waiting to go home again was a bit like waiting for Christmas." The children still seemed perturbed. "You wait and wait and you think that Christmas is so far away, and it will never come but it does, in the end. Waiting is OK."

Miss Long's face crinkled into a smile as she tried to fight back tears. Her patient Virginie had now explained to her the impact of her bizarre childhood, and Miss Long had felt devastated not to have realized at the time, the pressure Virginie had been under. It seemed particularly cruel that a child who had waited, as she put it, to be free of the restraints of caring for her mother, had then had to wait in prison for such a large percentage of her adult life to be able to escape and start living.

"I think my life was meant to be like this," Virginie continued, more to herself than anyone else. "I have learnt so much from my life and my experiences. I am glad for everything that has happened to me. And I am very content. Not everyone has had to do so much waiting as me, so they find it very hard when they need to be patient, even for a short while. But I am not afraid of anything now."

Miss Long drove Virginie back to her digs and gave her a care package of sandwiches and cake. "I just wish that I could have helped you more," she said to Virginie again, with such regret in her voice.

"You did help me," smiled Virginie. "You told me you admired my mum. She was a very special person and I was glad to look after her. And one day when I die I will see her again and say that I loved her. I never did say that her and I wish that I had."

"She was fiercely proud of you," Miss Long finished as Virginie got out of the car. "I am not sure that many people understood her as well as you did."

Virginie had a faraway look in her eyes, a look Miss Long remembered with a shiver. It was the look that Virginie had had soon

PEOPLE PERSON

after she had been arrested. It was a look of quiet purpose, resolution. It made her look wonderful and terrible, like an avenging angel.

"It is not right to take a life," Virginie whispered. "I think I will see her soon."

Then she was gone into the house and Miss Long drove away, not daring to call after her.

ALEX SPEAR

PEOPLE PERSON

Chapter Six

As agreed, I returned to the Keeping Britain Great office. Pathaway's mother let me in a bit more graciously this time and said, "He'll be glad one's come back; they don't often."

When I was admitted into his stuffy office, I saw that today, Pathaway had visitors. Sitting in front of his desk was Rita, of the impressively wrinkled hands, and hovering nearby, unsure whether to sit or stand, was Irene of the purple hair. They both recognized me immediately from the jury.

"Hello, dears!" Rita grinned, her teeth as yellow as ever. "We were on the murder trial together except our verdict was slung out," she explained to Pathaway.

"Murder trial?" he said with some suspicion.

I stiffened. The deceit of pretending not to have known Virginie well before the trial still left me confused and stressed sometimes. Making an effort to stay calm, I worked out quickly that Pathaway had as much to conceal as I did. He had to pretend to know Mathilde less well than he in fact had, and he had effectively distanced himself from her and her family when they had become a liability. If, as we suspected, he had been quite relieved when she had died—he may have even been considering helping her on her way himself—then it was likely that his interest in the case was more to keep himself in the clear.

I remembered him at the trial now, sitting in the public gallery throughout, making frantic notes of everything that was said.

"Yes, all three of us were on the jury together," I said. "The first jury, that is." I was trying not to stare at Pathaway, but he had something of a grin appearing on his face and that couldn't be good. Now I thought about it, why on earth had he been so keen to keep notes of the evidence? What had been his interest in who had killed the Medusa?

Irene broke our silence. "Are you helping with the cause?" she asked me. She beamed when I nodded. "So important to get young people involved. That's what Fred says."

Pathaway looked irritated not to have been the quoted guru.

"Fred?" I must have looked blankly at her. She seemed to think I would know who he was.

"My husband! I met him on the jury. Don't you remember? He's a council member, and he's going to help Reginald. Why shouldn't he stand? It just isn't fair that all the voices of local people who want him to represent them aren't heard when they are shouting for change."

A shiver ran down my spine. Shouting for change was a favourite Pathaway slogan. Irene was so easy to brainwash, the dozy cow. And of course, the old boy she had fallen for on the jury was just the sort to become a counsellor and want to help a small-minded group like Keeping Britain Great. I remembered his bigoted views. I could hear his self-assured voice pontificating from over eight years before: 'If a country couldn't manage itself, we'd be on hand to advise, you know. Experience.' I could easily extrapolate his views on immigration.

"I remember the first jury's verdict," Pathaway said, his smile returning. "You believed the poor woman had in fact been attacked and killed by a young foreign boy, name of Patel. You had the right idea. The second jury found the daughter guilty, but I always had my doubts." His eyes were shining as he looked at me. "I've mentioned him to you before. Needs to be taught a lesson. Still rather too cocky."

I fought to keep my facial expression neutral. "I remember you saying so, sir." I wanted to change the subject before my discomfort became apparent. "Oh, and I meant to ask, what's the priority in the run up to the election? Should we go leafleting, talking to people, or should we focus more on an event?"

"Ooh, an event sounds exciting," Rita crooned. "A big public rally with musicians. It would be like the sixties."

PEOPLE PERSON

"Not the sixties. Much too liberal," Pathaway shuddered. "Eighties more like, with Margaret Thatcher leading the country to greatness—the finest woman that ever breathed."

"Don't you do something with events, Felix?" Irene asked suddenly.

How on earth did she know that?

"I thought it was you working in Chariot. I've walked past and almost said 'Hello.' You were there with loads of balloons, a good few months ago now. Do you remember? One of your colleagues said you were organising an event for that night, so I didn't want to disturb you."

"Oh, I didn't see you." This was horrible. I hated the thought of my real life and my pretended allegiance to Keeping Britain Great getting mixed up like this. I also hated the thought of using my one talent for the good of Pathaway and his bigoted cronies.

But it was too late. It seemed to be all settled as far as they were concerned. I found myself agreeing to organise a large street party in aid of their bigoted cause. It would have a wartime theme to support our continued military presence in Afghanistan and to promote a return to old-fashioned values (ha, such as homophobia and racism.) It was to take place four weeks before the election, by which time Fred was to have arranged for Keeping Britain Great to be able to stand, giving us enough time to whip the locals into a racist frenzy before they voted.

I hoped all this reverse psychology would eventually pay off. I was starting to wonder whether my efforts would really help the right side win or whether I was just kidding myself.

ALEX SPEAR

PEOPLE PERSON

Chapter Seven

Gina let me visit her in her new lodgings. She told me to come on a Monday when the restaurant was closed.

Tracy let me in just as she was going out and showed me to the kitchen out the back. It was all brushed stainless-steel surfaces, scrupulously clean, although unlike the restaurant I worked in, it didn't have any of the industrial mod-cons like a massive dishwasher. It had a charming, homespun air.

Gina was at the stove making herself just about the cheapest meal I've ever seen. Potatoes and nettles. She calls it 'champ,' which sounds to me more like something you'd feed to horses.

"Hey. Would you like some?" she offered with a smile.

"Obviously not." I made a face at her horrible food.

The jury was still out (ha ha) on whether we were a couple again. We both wanted to stop the Keeping Britain Great party for good. Without Mathilde Harper, they had been severely weakened in this area for years, and it had seemed at one point that they had folded altogether. But now, the recession was biting, and the locals, who included plenty of plasterers, builders, painter-decorators and plumbers, were struggling for trade. Family incomes were going down and people were starting to feel nervous. Swinton was looking for a more aggressive type of leadership than previously and was ready for slightly less charity being shown to others. Extreme views were being tolerated. Minority groups were once again being used as scapegoats for the difficulties faced by locals. Keeping Britain Great had gradually rallied and by now, large numbers of voters were quite open about their affiliation.

"What have you found out?" Gina turned from the stove to ask me.

My infiltration of KBG was paying off. Dropping my voice even though the house was empty, I brought her up to speed. Once again, Reginald Pathaway was aiming for the respectability of having a council member as a champion. His party was not currently allowed to stand in elections due to its discriminatory membership policy, but right up until her death Mathilde had been fighting for their recognition. Her murder had set them back years, but now, it seemed that once again they had secured a friend on the inside. With Fred, Irene's husband, on the council, the elected members seemed to genuinely believe that all points of view should be heard and were softening to Pathaway's manipulation. The likely result was that by the time of the next council elections, Pathaway would be standing, and a good number of local people would use a vote for him in the hope that he could restore their former good standard of living.

Gina's face was very serious and slightly drawn. She received this news and continued to stir the concoction in the pot before her. I could see she was planning our next move.

"Listen, Gina, forget the champ. Why don't you sit down in the restaurant and I'll make you some lunch?"

I loved to cook for her. Tracy had already said we could eat anything we wanted from the kitchen to supplement Gina's pitiful wages.

I found some amazing dark green watercress in the fridge and blitzed it to make her a soup. I wanted her to taste that iron-rich purity.

Gina's passion fired everyone, even those as lazy as me. I wasn't quite as apathetic as I used to be, having experienced a bit of homophobia from people who should know better. Reginald Pathaway seemed to give quite ordinary, rational people a channel for their hidden bigoted beliefs or else the beliefs weren't in them until he implanted them. I couldn't be sure, but either way, all forward-thinking people in the area needed to keep him out.

PEOPLE PERSON

After I'd quickly cooked the soup, I rested the pan in a load of ice I'd scraped from the freezer. I wanted the watercress to stop cooking, so it wouldn't lose that amazing color.

The elections were due in the summer. We had eight short weeks to get local people thinking. Gina had always been a passionate 'anti-Path' as we called ourselves, and she asked Bobby Patel to give us a hand as well. My friend Rachel didn't mind helping.

Even with her new name, Gina rather than Virginie, plenty of local people remembered her and the notorious case of the murderous daughter. There was no way Virginie could publicly work for any local politician without making them very unpopular. For my part, I didn't want to lose the advantage I had by pretending to side with Pathaway. It was useful to find out what he was up to, so we agreed to continue with me as a sort of low-budget double agent.

So, that was how Bobby ended up standing. From behind the scenes I coached him in how to be popular. Lazy, laid-back Felix finally had a cause, a calling. Gina never came out and said, 'If we defeat Pathaway, I'll love you again,' but that was how it felt.

I set the watercress soup in front of Gina. She started to eat it, spoonful by spoonful, while we talked about our plan with our words and our relationship with our eyes.

That was the main thing that I wanted to sort out. I had slept with Charmaine years ago but had never really discussed it with Gina. If she had slept with someone else while she was locked up, I guessed I deserved it. But I wished we could talk it out.

She ate all the soup. My eyebrows nearly shot off the top of my head with surprise at this, but I didn't say anything. It felt like a big thing going on, and I had a hunch what it was about. As I cleared her plate and spoon, I dropped a kiss on her forehead and said, "I'm sorry."

I stood behind her, hardly daring to breathe. Would she know what the hell I was talking about? Would she accept my apology and move on?

Eventually she said in a firm voice, "What else have you got?"

I raced into the kitchen and set about making her my special mushroom risotto, an enormous, creamy dish that everyone loved but no one could ever finish when I made it at Chariot. It took ages to make, and I felt my fervent prayers as I stirred and stirred. *Please, please, love me again.*

I brought it through and set it down. I showered the glistening rice with Parmesan shards. She started to eat … and eat.

She went back to our plan on how we would promote Bobby Patel in the area. I babbled on, wondering if we would get back to the matter I wanted to resolve. I offered all the skills I had in promotion and in creating that wild party feeling in people. From behind the scenes, I would style Bobby as a fun, life-affirming alternative to the doom and gloom Keeping Britain Great were pushing. A vote for Bobby was as much of a statement as a vote for Pathaway was. Neither could get enough of the votes to win, but it would provide a way for locals to demonstrate that they were fed up with the main parties and which way they swung would impact the issues that the ultimate winner would focus on. Bobby would stand as an independent candidate under the banner of 'Vote for the Party Party party.' He was all about being young and passionate and something of a heartthrob. Guys wanted to *be* him, and girls wanted to be *with* him.

Hell, we could have been separated at birth.

But right now, I wasn't feeling much like a heartthrob. All I wanted was for my childhood sweetheart to forgive me. She eventually finished the great plateful of risotto, visibly slowing down by the end. I cleared her bowl and her fork and said it again, "I'm sorry."

She said, "What's for pudding?"

I brought her all four that were on the specials board: warm brownie, apple pie, fruit salad, and ice cream. She scraped them all into one bowl and gulped them down in great spoonfuls, not tasting, staring straight ahead. Then, when there was nothing left in the bowl but the slightest scrape of pale yellow, melted ice cream, she rose carefully and walked slightly unsteadily to the ladies', disappearing inside for about ten minutes. When she came out again, she was white as a sheet and her beautiful hair was damp around the edges where she'd clearly splashed her face with cold water.

I sat her down with a black coffee, sat down opposite her, and said, "Baby, I am so, *so* sorry." And when I thought about her never being able to forgive me it made me start to tear up just a bit, and I never cry. I put my head on my arms and just felt the saddest I think I ever have. She reached out a hand and put it on top of my head, and said, "OK."

Later, she told me the reason she had kissed a girl in prison was to get back at me for the whole Charmaine thing. It had felt like a sort of revenge, but she had not felt much better afterwards. She had mostly

PEOPLE PERSON

wanted me to understand how much I had hurt her. I could comprehend it now. She had made me grow up enough to get that kind of empathy.

ALEX SPEAR

PEOPLE PERSON

Chapter Eight

I had found the missing diary at Keeping Britain Great headquarters. I was having a snoop around Reg's office, duster in hand, while he had popped to the post box. The front cover said 2008 in gold letters.

I couldn't resist opening it up about halfway through and having a peak at an entry. It was as incriminating as we could have imagined. Mathilde had expressed her fear about the man she was now dangerously close to.

"11th May. He's got a way of assuming he owns me. It was exciting at first, but it has started to feel a bit sinister. He touches me in public like it's his right. He feels he can do what he likes with me."

Less than four months later, she was dead. I had always thought that Gina had killed her mother, but that was because she, Gina, had also believed that she had. Supposing Gina only thought she had killed her mother and someone else had?

This was the diary we needed all right. It was the last one before Mathilde died, and the fact it was missing from her house and had turned up in the Keeping Britain Great headquarters in Reg's personal drawer needed explaining. I couldn't wait to get it back to Gina and read it in detail. I shoved the diary under my shirt and tucked it into my jeans, pulling out a blank one that Gina had suggested I use as a replacement. I dropped it into the drawer and pulled a few other odds and ends over it. He would eventually realize it was a decoy, but it would buy us time.

Reg came back into his office suddenly. Thank God, I had already pushed the drawer shut. He narrowed his eyes at me. "What are you doing?" he demanded.

"Just tidying up a bit," I said lamely, moving a few papers from the desk together into a pile. He went and sat in his chair and switched on his computer moodily. He didn't really suspect me. He never thought a girl could do anything bad, not really. His main concern was Bobby Patel.

He had Rita typing up the minutes of his last public meeting where he had publicly condemned Bobby as the son of an immigrant family and therefore somehow at odds with the values local people held dear. Even Rita had looked a bit bemused by this one, but she obediently typed up the great man's words. And he had Irene in the kitchen re-washing all his tea cups and spoons, ready for his next planning session. They were clean. His mum did all the washing up straight after any meeting, but he always looked back through the cups and decided they weren't clean enough. Then, he got either me or Irene to re-wash them, sometimes more than once.

Reg asked me to come and dust the window behind him, and I was glad of the distraction. Him catching me in one of his cabinets had been an awkward moment.

I was aware of him opening the drawer, and he must have been satisfied when he had seen the replacement diary in there because he quietly shut the drawer again without a word. I breathed again and started to dust.

As I reached up with the long-handled feather duster to do the little individual window segments at the top, I thought I felt something on my ass. I turned and looked down, and I could have sworn Reg had hurriedly pulled his hand back. Dear God, was he groping me? And even more pathetic, pretending he hadn't?

Until that point, I'd say I was a bit sexist myself. Maybe that was how I managed to blend in so well with Reg and his ilk. It's a funny thing how, as a young woman, I never really thought of myself as female, and for some reason I was able to think of other women as being a bit on the weedy, emotional side. I was really surprised when a girl could do anything clever or difficult. I never felt much like a girl

PEOPLE PERSON

myself and didn't really equate other women being badly treated with anything that affected me and my life.

His grope had brought me down to earth. He saw me as female, all right, and not his equal.

We needed to sort him out and fast. He was such a freak. A nasty, misogynistic man. And, as I was beginning to suspect, a dangerous one.

ALEX SPEAR

PEOPLE PERSON

Chapter Nine

It was my favourite kind of weather; warm with a breeze. The bunting fluttered, and the England flags whipped on their flag poles. I was struggling to erect trestle tables ready for the food donated by my restaurant. My hands were sweaty, and the splintered wood was slipping out of my hands.

I was nervous. The plan was that when all the locals were seated at this street party full of food and booze and waiting for Keeping Britain Great to do speeches and so on, Bobby Patel and his supporters would conga through the area, and the residents would see how handsome and full of life he was and how much fun all his supporters were having. The Party Party party would hijack the stage to make a speech of optimism and the future, and they would win hearts and minds.

It was a risky strategy that Gina had cooked up. The main danger, of course, was that the rough and aggressive contingent of Keeping Britain Great would start a fight with the fiery, young men on Bobby's side. As Anti-Paths, we were angry and ready to resist the oppressors with force, if necessary. I needed to manage this very carefully, as any trouble would reflect badly on both sides. But I knew from my insider information that Reginald Pathaway had said privately that any violence from his supporters would connect him in people's minds with the fascist groups he was so careful to distance himself from. He needed the day to remain peaceable as much as we did.

Gina had explained to Bobby how he was to prepare his supporters on the day. "Talk to them about peace and co-operation," she urged. "We retain the moral high ground by listening to our opponent's point of view. Then we rationally explain why they're wrong."

Bobby had studied marketing at Swinton Uni, and he sometimes came out with these hilarious expressions I'd not heard before. That morning he said, "Yeah, yeah, our, like, *unique selling point* is that we are fun and reasonable, not like the 'establishment,' controlling or whatever."

I set out some enormous bowls on the tables and began to fill them from catering packs. Potato salad, prawn cocktail, and coleslaw. The weather wasn't due to be warm enough to make things go off for a while, but I set the bowl of prawn cocktail on a dish of ice cubes to be on the safe side.

A few people were starting to arrive. Irene and Fred turned up arm in arm, Irene in a pretty summer dress. Fred sat down at a table with ramrod-straight posture, and Irene started running around helping me with food.

I made sure I kept giving Reginald big tankards of the real ale we'd had donated by the local brewery. I'd prayed his red, bloodshot nose meant he was a boozer, and it looked as if I'd been right. He kept making a pretend fuss about not having another drink, then accepting after all with the "you twisted my arm" stuff. I kept topping up his glass and he kept glugging it down. Perfect.

Two of Rita's grandsons were there and Irene's son from her first marriage … their shaved heads gleaming in the pale British sun. I don't exactly avoid lads like that—in Swinton, you'd be forever crossing the road—but I would certainly play down my cocky gay walk in front of them, and there's no way I would hold Gina's hand or give her a kiss until they were well out of sight.

The three of them had helped set up the little, raised platform where Reg would do his speech later. And now, they were standing around having some beers. Rita's grandsons both had their England football shirts on. Irene's son had on a Kappa jacket covered with the little, round holes that 'hot rocks' of skunk make; all his clothes were marked. Mason, I think his name is. He's a scary bugger. He's a drug dealer and general thug in the area.

PEOPLE PERSON

Reg was standing on stage and spoke into the mike. We were deafened by the sudden feedback noise.

I slipped behind a sort of tent that had been set up for the generator and other equipment. I got out my mobile to update Gina, who was organizing from her room at Tracy's.

"Reg's going to make his speech around four. He's already quite trollied. Get Bobby to come round before then."

"*Reg?*" Gina's voice sounded scathing. "We call him Pathaway, remember?"

"Yeah, well, I've got to blend in, haven't I?"

I could tell she wasn't impressed, but she said she'd organize Bobby's interjection as we'd agreed.

When it happened, it couldn't have worked out better. Crowds of people had come out to enjoy an old-fashioned street party, whether they were fans of Pathaway's or not. They were all sitting at the long tables in the street under the bunting. When the band had paused its playing and Reg was just getting up on to the stage, looking self-important, I sent the text to Gina. It read simply '*Now.*'

Bobby ambled across the stage followed by a conga line of young students dressed up in mad costumes: body painted, sequined, cowboy-hatted, feather boa-wearing kids just kept on coming and coming. There were hundreds of them. The band started to play a Mardi Gras-style tune, and all the spectators got up to dance as well. They thought it was all part of the street party. Cameras were flashing like crazy, people were whooping and whistling, and Reg stood in the middle of it all going beetroot.

He had to try to look like he was still in charge. He raised a hand and said, "Please," but could hardly be heard over the din. He looked like a proper Canute. A passing girl caught him up in her pink feather boa and danced around him. As Reg tried to extricate himself from the girl and her feathers, Bobby grabbed the mike and shouted, "Yeah! Party Party party! A vote for me is a vote for love, peace, and tolerance!"

They unfurled a banner with a Bobby Patel slogan, "Be Nice," over the front of the stage, obliterating the Union Jacks that were pinned up.

It was all over for Reg. He was too drunk to stand up for himself. He flounced off the stage and couldn't be coaxed back on by his supporters. Things couldn't have gone better. In an entirely peaceful and popular way, Bobby had used the Keeping Britain Great platform to chip away at their power and had got the crowd applauding for him instead. His good-looking, young face was captured by the camcorder that had been set up on the tripod, and one of our lot rushed to project it onto the side of the equipment tent. The band carried on playing the more upbeat music that seemed appropriate for the Party Party party, and people danced to it all afternoon.

PEOPLE PERSON

Chapter Ten

"Ooh, I still can't believe it!"

Gina was squealing, and I couldn't stop grinning. Back at her house with some of my friends, we congratulated ourselves on a brilliant day. With more sabotage planned for Keeping Britain Great, we were full of the thrill of success and optimism. We felt invincible.

Hugging each other and downing mugs full of cheap, red wine, we celebrated. We were going to a club, something Gina had never gotten around to doing in her turbulent young adulthood. She was thrilled by my and Bobby's descriptions of how the rally had gone from our separate vantage points. We were all in the mood to celebrate.

Gina put on a new dress: black taffeta with a silver satin bow round her waist. I say 'new,' but of course, it had come from a charity shop for a few pounds. Rachel had begged Gina to let her put some makeup on her, something she never bothered with. I wanted to see her in makeup too.

She sat down at Rachel's dressing table with the three mirrors. Her face was slightly flushed in the low light, and she had a funny, shy, little smile.

Rachel advanced with an enormous powder brush. I don't bother with makeup, myself. Never got into it, being a bit on the butch side, but I know roughly where all the products go. Rachel dusted Gina's face all over, so it became a lightly powdered confection, then added a little colour to the apples of her cheeks. She sternly instructed Gina to close her eyes gently, "Don't screw them up," and lightly brushed a shimmery, slate-colored powder over her eyelids. A slight combing of mascara made her dark eyelashes even longer, and a slick of peach lip gloss made her mouth look edible.

Rachel whirled her round in her chair, so I could see the finished effect. I'd always known Gina was beautiful, but suddenly, the effect was heightened. Her subtle features became stronger, and her wise, frank face became soft focus and adorable.

I'll always remember her like that.

"I do love you," I whispered, giving her a kiss.

"I love you too," she smiled. I ran my fingers through her hair, close-cropped and slightly tousled, as if her sleep had been troubled.

Gina's mobile rang. She answered it without a thought, her face flushed with happiness at the evening we were to have.

As soon as she heard the voice on the phone, her face fell.

I heard her trying to assert herself to the pushy caller, whoever he was. She tried to get a word in edgeways: "... But Mason, listen ... Twyla and I, we never ..."

I grabbed her phone and pushed the 'end call' button. She squeaked.

"Who was that?"

"Oh, some awful man who followed me when I left the prison," Gina was quavering. She looked terrified. "I didn't realize he is the partner of my cellmate, Twyla. She told him ..." Gina trailed off, looking incredibly guilty.

"Well, forget about all that now, like the police advised you. Put it all behind you."

She couldn't shake it off. "I never thought I'd make old bones, Felix. I just feel that my story is nearly over."

I had one more thing to do that night. I arranged to take Rachel to the Keeping Britain Great headquarters. I was to meet Gina and Bobby later outside the club.

Rachel was posing as a student reporter and took the camcorder round to interview Pathaway. I was there to get him drunk. I took along two bottles of champagne and prayed he'd underestimate the intelligence of two girls.

PEOPLE PERSON

I had a key to let us into the offices. He was kind of slumped against his desk, his mother clucking over him.

"See if you can talk some sense into him," she grumbled, leaving us to it.

"Great rally, Mr. Pathaway!" I fawned.

"Rubbish," he slurred. "Hijacked. Mongrel boy. Laughing stock."

"This is Rachel from the student newspaper," I said loudly, ignoring his self-pity. "She's come to do a piece on you. She wasn't at the rally. Maybe you can fill her in on what happened?"

She held up her camcorder and started filming his confused face. "Perhaps you could let me know what the theme of your speech was, Mr. Pathaway?" she asked. "And then take us through the issues you'll be highlighting when you stand in the local elections in a fortnight."

She had him completely charmed. Once he'd established she hadn't been at the rally, Pathaway became a great, leering ham, telling a complete fabrication of his performance that day, posing and pontificating for Rachel's camera. I surreptitiously poured him a glass of champagne and placed it in his hand. He started to sip it almost without noticing.

She let him ramble on about immigration, Christian morals, family values, and how gays and single mothers had caused the breakdown of society. I kept topping up his glass. He was too far gone to notice that she and I were still on our first. When the second bottle of champagne was drained, Rachel finished up her interview and made a big show of turning off the camera.

"Thank you so much, Mr. Pathaway. My fellow students will find that enlightening," she breathed, batting her eyelashes for England.

"Call me Reg," he perved, openly staring down the top of her shirt.

Just outside his line of vision I managed to press the 'record' button on the Dictaphone in my inside pocket without him seeing.

"Now that we're 'off the air,' Rachel sighed, brazenly tugging at the top of her shirt to make it fall open just a little more at the front, "tell me about the man behind the politics. What's the secret of your success in this area? You must have had to be very ruthless."

"I don't contemplate failure," he slurred. "I deal with the opposition. *Mathilde and Bobby and whoever I need to.* I don't intend to lose."

Rachel and I both fought not to give away the tiniest reaction when we heard this. It had been an almost throwaway remark, and Pathaway seemed to have shocked himself with it. It sobered him up slightly. He got back onto much less contentious topics. But he had said it, and I had recorded him saying it. *I deal with the opposition. Mathilde and Bobby ....*

It was enough. In my blood, I knew it was enough. With Mathilde's diary that showed how brutal a man Pathaway had been behind closed doors, this half confession on tape would surely make the people round here question the original verdict at the controversial double trial that had eventually found Virginie Harper guilty of her mother's murder.

Wouldn't it?

We had to try.

We excused ourselves as quickly as we dared, and I took the Dictaphone round to Charmaine's for safe keeping. She was going to speak to her friends in the local court again about process and the best way to get the police involved. There could be only one outcome this time and that was for Reginald Pathaway to go to prison for the murder he had committed. We must also prevent the second murder he planned and get Gina pardoned, so she would be able to live as a free woman in the town she had given so much for. This time, I knew it would work. We would not fail again as we had failed with the jury.

This time, the right people would win, and my Gina and I would live happily ever after.

PEOPLE PERSON

Chapter Eleven

As soon as I saw Charmaine at the police station, I knew something was terribly wrong. "You haven't heard, then?" were the first words she said to me; words with the power to make my bowels grow icy-cold.

We saw it on the CCTV footage: snowy grey images without sound. My precious Gina cornered in an alley and stabbed by no fewer than four masked attackers: huge, burly men, one with white supremacist tattoos, two in England football shirts. The hands flailing backwards and forwards. The jerky movements of Gina's torso as the knifepoints slid into her. Her innocent face suddenly screwed up in pain and terror. The way she sank to the ground and the long minutes as the four watched her to make sure they had done enough. One of them snapped his head round as if he had heard a noise and they all fled.

Charmaine drove me and Rachel to Swinton General Hospital. I was beyond being calmed down and Rachel was shaking too much to drive.

We sat on plastic chairs. Gina was fighting for her life, and no one could see her while she was in intensive care. The WPC outside the door said that there would be plenty of time for me to identify the masked attackers in the CCTV footage later. The police had a good idea who the men were anyway—they had been after Mason for a long time.

I was exhausted from crying. "Why?" was all I could croak.

"I've heard from the police that Mason found out about Virginie and his wife carrying on in prison," Charmaine said. "He didn't take it too well. He hates dykes, and obviously, he hates the thought of his wife being unfaithful. Word is, the double whammy made him swear he'd kill the culprit. Twyla's lucky to be inside where he can't get at her."

The doctors told me it was touch and go. I could go in and see Virginie for a minute as she was very weak and might not survive the night. I crept into her side room where she was sitting on the commode, hooked up to a big monitoring machine with tubes and wires. Her face was ashen and running with sweat. Her little stomach was bandaged round and round where they had managed to stop the bleeding, but they warned her she would need surgery for her insides when she was strong enough ... that was, if she didn't die first. This battle might prove too much for my hero, my Virginie of grit and integrity.

She was struggling to speak. "You must tell the police," she managed. "Mason. He admitted to killing Mummy. He was crowing about it, when he thought he'd also killed me. 'Mother and daughter, I am the king!' he was telling his mates. Reginald Pathaway paid him to do it. Mummy was starting to question their nasty Fascist policies, so they arranged for her to die to shut her up. You must get Mason locked away and Pathaway too."

"I will tell them, my darling," I soothed, briefly reflecting that it would be impossible to prove after all this time, unless Mason's friends would squeal. "But you forget about it now, you rest."

She was clinging to life, those blazing eyes somewhat flattened and dimmed, but still beautiful. I held Virginie in my arms and told her a fairy tale.

"Once there was a girl who could only tell the truth. She and her brother were imprisoned in a horrible, ruined old castle by an evil witch and a mad, old wizard. The wizard taught the girl how to make potions, but then he died. The witch was strangely controlled by an evil king in the area. The girl fell in love with a lazy prince."

She raised her pale face and gave me one of her saucy grins. "Did the prince rescue her from the castle and the evil witch?"

PEOPLE PERSON

"Well, the lazy prince sort of tried to rescue the girl but didn't manage it, and then, the girl saved herself by killing the witch. Then the girl was imprisoned again and tormented by a monster who was really a beautiful mother under a curse. And the girl carried on telling the truth even though she was imprisoned. She was slandered, and the prince that she loved heard and believed that she had been untrue. But she managed to break the spell and turn the monster back into the beautiful mother she had been and set the other prisoners free in their hearts. Then, she escaped from the prison and returned home."

"And then? What happened to the girl and the prince?"

"Well, the girl had to go through all the possessions in the ruined castle and break the spell the evil witch and mad wizard had put on the place. She made her potions and the kingdom became joyful again. She found out that the evil witch had been imprisoned by the mad wizard years before, and she had been an ordinary girl who had become cursed when her daughter had been born. Finally, the prince and the girl who could only tell the truth both attended a masked ball, and after a series of misunderstandings they were reconciled. They fought the evil forces in the kingdom and deposed the king. They brought harmony and security to the kingdom."

Her eyes were full of tears. "They did, didn't they. And then?"

"Well, it's a fairy tale, so they got married and lived happily ever after."

"But this is real life," she said sadly. I started to realise that the saucy grin on her face was frozen, and her skin was turning white and waxy. Virginie was speaking to me inside my head but her lips weren't moving. Her slightly oversized mouth was pulled back in a snarl and her teeth were exposed. "This is no fairy tale. They didn't get married and live happily ever after even though they had brought down the evil king. The lawless elements in the kingdom had heard the rumours of the girl being unfaithful and they butchered her. And the lazy prince who could make everyone happy never laughed again."

As if in slow motion, I saw the medical team rush into the room in response to the beeping coming from Virginie's life support machines. A kind, male nurse took me by the shoulder and gently propelled me out of the side room and back to the plastic chairs of the waiting area where Rachel held me, the two of us bowled over by our grief. Charmaine had gone, and I realised in that moment I hated her, and I hated myself more.

I keep seeing my Virginie's lifeless body lying there. She had her hands neatly folded across her lap. Her close-cropped hair was slightly tousled, as if her sleep was troubled, and she seemed even thinner than I remembered. Very thin but not fragile … filled with quiet purpose. I remember her calm, steady gaze rarely directed at me.

PEOPLE PERSON

Chapter Twelve

Later that year, I appeared in court to give evidence about Mason and Pathaway and the facts I knew about their involvement in the arranged killing of Virginie's mother. There were complicated legal processes involved but the conspiracy charges were the most compelling. Mason was already looking at a life sentence for the attempted murder of Virginie Harper, known as Gina, of Swinton.

As I started the long drive up to our new home by the seaside, I wondered briefly who inherited the riches of her medicinal garden, surrounded by its chain-link cage. I don't go near the murder house now, and out of respect for Virginie, I don't see Charmaine at all either. So, Swinton held less for me now, and I suppose it was natural to look for somewhere else to live, a fresh start away from all the bad memories.

The night was closing fast around me and I turned my headlights on full beam, illuminating the empty dual carriageway. In a flash, I saw the burning eyes of a rabbit flash across the road, enormous brown eyes holding my gaze in an expression of innocence, then gone safely to central reservation. I swore at the near miss, realising I had been speeding in my haste to get back.

The car phone chirruped, and I smacked the inside of the ceiling in my haste to get it turned on to hands-free. "Virginie? I'll be there in a couple of hours, then we can start our weekend."

I loved her crisp voice with the sarcasm, the warmth. "The beer is in the fridge, and I'm making your favourite for dinner," she laughed.

I groaned. "Please tell me it's not that awful champ."

"My appointment with the doctor went well. Thanks for asking," she teased.

"Oh, sorry. I forgot to ask. That's great news. Your stitches have all healed now, after the op? Wow, you have done so well. You have bounced back pretty quickly, considering what you've been through."

"Must be all the champ."

"It's still not worth eating it, even for its alleged healing properties." I was grinning like an idiot. My heart was full of joy at the thought of being with her. I glared at the sat-nav. Still an hour and fifty to go. I put my foot down and barrelled along the empty road.

"And for dessert..." she continued.

"Yes?" She had my attention now.

She gave a small, saucy giggle. "Just wait and see."

~ THE END ~

About Alex Spear

Alex Spear loves traveling the world listening for stories. Born in London, she now lives with her wife by the sea. Many, many decades have passed since Alex was at school but she still gets told off for being easily distracted. She will typically be writing two novels, a blog and a TV script all at once while reading half a dozen novels (none from beginning to end) while talking to good friends online, on the phone, and to her cat. Alex says, "I am passionate about women and my mission is to tell our stories. The power of female relationships, from friendships to love affairs and everything in between, is the true history of the world. I want women to enjoy themselves more, and to look after themselves at least as well as they do everyone else."

✤ OUT ✤

If you have enjoyed **RESTRAINT**
please look for ALEX SPEAR's novel **OUT** from
Shadoe Publishing:
We have a chapter here for your enjoyment.

PART ONE

I had entirely forgotten how to dance, but I only had to follow her. She could dance for both of us.

Simoine de Beauvouir
The Blood of Others

 Standing outside the clinic, making sure I couldn't be seen, I turned my phone back on, and frowned. Missed call? I checked the number: House Phone. Before I could even return the call, my phone buzzed and flashed into life again, and it was Colin. My stomach dropped when I heard his voice. Colin, the control freak, always in charge, sounded like he was out of his mind with terror.
 "Colin? What's the – "
 "Lydia? Half the house has just – oh, God, it's so awful – "
 "What? What's happened?" With a furtive look round, I ran to get away from the ambulance sirens.
 Colin's voice was stretched with panic. "Where are you, Lydia? I didn't know where anyone was, I didn't know what to do..."
 I hesitated, not wanting to lie. "Tell you later. What is it, though?"
 "The crazy room – Sarah's room – it's fallen down. It's just collapsed."

✦ ALEX SPEAR ✦

Chapter One

She looked terrified. I have that effect.

Lydia was flushed with embarrassment, right down over the neck and possibly as far as her tiny breasts. She had the kind of bone-white skin that often flares with eczema or mottles with freckles, but she had neither.

She must have grabbed the towel when I had knocked on her door. Her white, English body was wrapped in holiday colours: flamingo pink, banana palm green, tequila sunset orange.

"Have you looked at many others?" she was asking.

"None so cheap." Only the slightest creping below the collar bone to show she was no longer in her teens. Proper woman's stomach, not too flat. "Can I see it?"

"Oh, yes, of course!" She made for the stairs.

I dropped my sports bag in the hallway, which was actually one side of the very small lounge, in the very small house. I pushed my bag gently against the flaking radiator. The bag contained my life, or what was left of it.

She was half-way up the narrow staircase. Her bottom was obligingly outlined by the clinging velour. "Or did you want a cup of tea first, Sarah?" She paused and looked over her shoulder; a slender, porcelain doll wearing an ice-lolly wrapper.

Tea?

The banisters gave a chipboard wobble and she pulled her hand away as if from a stove.

Why was she stalling?

Of course. Suddenly, I understood her nerves, her rush to the door to let me in. The room was cheap, and she was desperate. It was going to be another dump. The three I'd seen that morning had been all but uninhabitable, and I'd been working down in price. This was the only one I could really afford. Dear God. How did I let things get so tragic?

"Nah. Let's see it."

We climbed to the phone box-sized landing together and she opened one of the four doors, singing out far too loudly, "there you go! Have a good look round! What do you think!" She stood aside to let me go in.

✦ OUT ✦

I could see why. This room ain't big enough for the both of us, sweet Lydia. It was really no bigger than the mean bed and MDF wardrobe pressed against the foot. (Do those doors even open?)

The room wasn't just far too small for sensible human occupation, it was also insane. By some deranged lack of planning or complete incompetence in the building, the walls were all at completely different gradients, not one of them perpendicular with the ceiling. You could have placed a marble in the doorway and it would have rolled miserably under the bed to the wall. Also, the reek of damp was as sharp as horse urine.

But.

The light.

Oh, the light.

The far wall was mostly window, apart from the mouldy lower third. There was another window in the right hand wall, which I calculated must be the end-of-terrace outside wall. Ancient crickle windows with rusted frames, bubbled with years of repainting. The room seemed to be more window than wall. It was a glasshouse, an observatory. To be in that room was to be bathed in the real light shining on this cruel planet. It was church when Jesus shows up.

I knelt on the bed and worshipped that view.

The view was postage-stamp gardens, plastic slides and black sacks. It was concrete roofs, it was estate walkways and the canal towpath furnished with street drinkers. It was a gang of kids on bikes, shouting and wheeling. It contained not a single tree. It was people. Life, community, other people, other people…I was exhausted by the sight of it already, yet desperate to watch it and watch it.

I've been alone for so long.

OK, easy there, Sarah. I wiped my eyes, quickly, knuckles dragged across before she could see.

"I'll take it," I growled, as she danced and shrieked in the background.

* * * * *

We had a real problem renting out the fourth room. It was built at crazy angles, and the same could be said of the last three tenants. Skanky Oliver rented the room a year, during which time, small explosions and smoke would emanate, until the summer day he disappeared. We broke the door down in the end, to find nothing but two empty suitcases, the bed up against the wall and on the stained carpet, the remnants of a modest but workable speed factory.

The second tenant we got in was a timid, intensely boring vegan girl. She filled our fridge with soya milk and sprouting mung beans, and woke us all up with her mad phone calls in the middle of the night. Christ knows who she rang. She spent hours at a time crying and going on and on about her guilt complex, her delicate and terribly complicated psyche. In the end, Pip had to ask her to go. Me and Colin kept out of it; we stayed in the kitchen while Pip sat her down in the lounge and gently explained that it wasn't working out. Pip's good at things like that. Besides, I had complicated matters by sleeping with the vegan a couple of times. I forget her name.

She had convictions, that was my downfall. What is it about a person so sure of their beliefs, that transforms them into the sexiest thing on earth? If I'm honest, it's butch women I really fancy, but it's pretty embarrassing admitting that these days. These days, even clinging resolutely to the old dyke uniform is kind of a fringe belief system, and it does things to me.

But a proper butch dyke is so hard to find, especially among girls of my age. It's like, you can be a lesbian, if you must, but you have to be feminine. At the very least you have to 'make the most of yourself.' Be honest, when is the last time you saw a butch lesbian on TV? They should be on the endangered species list. It won't be long before the last few get Gok Wang'ed or whatever, and I'll have no-one left to fall in love with.

The most recent tenant was a big biker guy, all leathers and body hair. He stayed a week, then got back together with his boyfriend, and left.

The crazy room stood empty, filled with light from the excessive windows, daring us to fill it again. We were really behind with the rent by now.

One night we were all in the lounge drinking, the way we do, when she rang. I grabbed the phone. Her voice was classic dyke: authoritative, cocky, with masculine inflection. Very crisp 'Ss. That kind of voice makes me go weak. I collapsed back into the chair with the phone cradled tenderly to my ear.

✤ OUT ✤

She said her name was Sarah. "I need a place to stay, very cheap."

"Where were you before, Sarah?" I did my best husky voice.

Our two kittens were fighting under the table. Jasper and Conran. I didn't name them, by the way.

For a second I thought she'd hung up. Then she did a bitter little laugh. "I…I lived with my partner, in her house, I mean. She died last year. Her parents took back the house and threw me out."

"…so you're single, are you, Sarah?" I said, nonchalantly.

Silence again. Jasper gave Conran a malicious swipe across the nose.

Maybe that wasn't such a sensitive thing to say. But, come on, she's not the one who died, you've got to move on at some point.

When she spoke again, she made her voice pierce right into my brain, like a really bad hangover.

"Have you ever lost someone you really loved?"

"No, I…" My English Lit teacher had told me I was like Emma in this regard. Some rubbish about nothing to vex me.

"Well, let me tell you, you don't think about being single, and going out on the scene, and sleeping around – you're too busy trying to hold it all together from one day to the next. Now, look, I need a cheap place to stay, when can I come and look at it." Not a request, an instruction. *God,* she was an old-school butch. Where have you been all my life, Sarah?

"Tomorrow morning" I said to the boys. If she's early enough, I'll let her in, show her the room. But I've got to go back to work – the sick pay's run out. And I can't be late again."

"You think she'll be alright?" Pip looked punch-drunk from the pageant of mad tenants we've had just recently.

"Oh, you know, fine." I breezed. "A bit older than us, I think."

"Let's hope she's better than that little vegan girl." This from Colin, his boyfriend, who was flicking through *Heat*. He was scanning the outfits on the celebs with a critical eye: glancing over each body, discarding, and moving on. Colin is a great dresser himself. He has a proper square jaw and a shaved head, and should be really good looking.

Pip was running around like a manic pixie, tidying up. Well, a pixie on steroids. Pip kind of looks like a stereotypical French chef, if you can imagine that. Tall and broad, soft belly, stubble, but where you'd

✤ ALEX SPEAR ✤

expect him to have a booming voice, he's hesitant, and obliging. He's not a French chef, he's actually Irish and doesn't really work. He's sort of a housewife to the rest of us. He never has any money, so he and Colin share a single room and Pip pays a bit when he can. Sometimes you forget Pip's in the room, which is an achievement for such a big man. He's always tidying up, which is great news for someone like me.

He lit some incense sticks, on either side of the massive china Buddha on the TV, then suddenly he was back with the hoover, and started darting in and out of our mismatched sofas. He manouvered the hoover carefully around Colin's feet, which didn't even twitch.

My lusting over Sarah's butch voice aside, we really needed someone normal to move in, who was good for the rent, and who would stay. Strictly speaking the crazy room wasn't big enough or safe enough to rent out, but we had to, to get Brian enough rent each month. My job in the call centre doesn't pay a huge amount, so I'm always strapped. We had to find a tenant who's not too picky to rent the crazy room, and they would have to hide from Brian when he comes round. Our doddery landlord might not have noticed the recent circus of tenant freaks, but he would soon notice the enormous hole in his finances if we didn't come up with some more rent, and quickly.

But we can't take just anyone. Our little household community is surprisingly sensitive. Each of us needs some certainty, even a bit of *kindness*, for our difference reasons. Maybe I need this place to work more than anyone. It's the only home I've known since I got kicked out of my parents', nearly three years ago now. I doubt whether anyone misses me. Skinny, scrawny, dykey, Lydia.

By the way, are you gay? Pretty much everyone in this story is gay, but if you're gay, you'd know that. If you're straight – hello there, and welcome.

I finally got Pip to sit down, but he was still sorting through the junk drawer from the kitchen. I mean he had pulled the whole thing out and had brought it to the lounge so he could sort all the old screws and chopsticks and biros while watching TV with me and Colin. His nimble fingers sorted through, removing grime, testing then rejecting a pen here and there, carefully organising the screws into little bags by size.

✦ OUT ✦

Pip's efforts made me feel quite exhausted, as I lounged on the smaller of the two sofas. Colin had some rubbish property programme on the TV, but I knew better than to complain, and I couldn't be bothered to read or anything. A trained gibbon could do my job in the call centre, but it still leaves me really drained, so in my off-time, I don't attempt anything more demanding than getting drunk.

Pip tapped me on the shoulder to give me a present from his junk drawer. "Here, Lydia. Instant lesbian kit. Convert any girl." He handed me an old necklace he'd rescued, onto which he'd threaded a bottle opener, and a mini nail clipper.

"Thanks, Pip." I slung it round my neck. Colin shushed us violently. We fell silent. Then, remembering I had work in the morning, I uncapped a new bottle of vodka, and set about getting wasted. I was feeling sick enough anyway, just going over and over in my head: *we're so behind with the rent.*

It hadn't helped that I'd phoned my mum that day, just to test the waters. I was considering asking her for a bit of money, but she just sounded so cold, so pleased I'd moved out, I steeled myself and made it just a social call. I heard all about my perfect sister and her husband, though. Even though my parents threw me out, I still end up trying to make them happy, and keep the details of my life from them. It's pretty depressing.

Colin sent Pip off into the kitchen to do the washing up. He's pretty bossy but he is a useful person to have in a house. He thinks about things I don't, like having a washing-up rota. He earns more than me, but he has to give most of it to his mum so it all gets cancelled out.

If he hadn't have been in a mood that night, I would have asked him if he thought his other half was OK. Pip's been looking very strained, lately.

We're *so* behind with the rent. I hate that quicksand feeling of getting deeper and deeper into debt. None of us have got anyone to turn to for financial help, all having burnt bridges in one way or another.

Please God, let her stay.

~End Sample Chapter of OUT~
For more go to www.Shadoepublishing.com to purchase
the complete book or for many other delightful offerings.

~ *Because a publisher should stand behind their authors*~

What do you do when you meet someone who changes everything you know about love and passion?

Paige Harlow is a good girl. She's always known where she was going in life: top grades, an ivy league school, a medical degree, regular church attendance, and a happy marriage to a man. So falling in love with her gorgeous roommate and best friend Alyssa Torres is no small crisis. Alyssa is chasing demons of her own, a medical condition that makes her an outcast and a family dysfunctional to the point of disintegration make her a questionable choice for any stable relationship. But Paige's heart is no longer her own. She must now battle the prejudices of her family, friends, and church and come to peace with her new sexuality before she can hope to win the affections of the woman of her dreams. But will love be enough?

www.shadoepublishing.com

~ *Because a publisher should stand behind their authors~*

REPRESENTED
K'ANNE MEINEL

Coming out is hard. Coming out in the public eye is even harder. People think they own a piece of you, your work, and your life, they feel they have the right to judge you. You lose not only friends but fans and ultimately, possibly, your career...or your life.

Cassie Summers is a Southern Rock Star; she came out so that she could feel true to herself. Her family including her band and those important to her support her but there are others that feel she betrayed them, they have revenge on their minds...

Karin Myers is a Rock Star in her own right; she is one of those new super promoters: Manager, go-to gal, agent, public relations expert, and hand-holder all in one. Her name is synonymous with getting someone recognized, promoted, and making money. She only handles particular clients though; she's choosy...for some very specific reasons.

Meeting Cassie at a party there is a definite attraction. She does not however wish to represent her despite her excellent reputation. She fights it tooth and nail until she is contractually required to do so. In nearly costs them more than either of them anticipated....their lives.

www.shadoepublishing.com

~ *Because a publisher should stand behind their authors~*

As I watch the wormhole start to close, I make one last desperate plea ... "Please? Please don't make me do this?" I whisper.
"You're almost out of time, Lily. Please, just let go?"
I look down at the control panel. I know what I have to do.

Lilith Madison is captain of the Phoenix, a spaceship filled with an elite crew and travelling through the Delta Gamma Quadrant. Their mission is mankind's last hope for survival.

But there is a killer on board. One who kills without leaving a trace and seems intent on making sure their mission fails. With the ship falling apart and her crew being ruthlessly picked off one by one, Lilith must choose who to trust while tracking down the killer before it's too late.

"A suspenseful...exciting...thrilling whodunit adventure in space...discover the shocking truth about what's really happening on the Phoenix" (Clarion)

www.shadoepublishing.com

~ *Because a publisher should stand behind their authors*~

INSIGHT

Jennis Slaughter

   When Delaney Delacroix is called to locate a missing girl, she never plans on getting caught up with a human trafficking investigation or with the local witch. Meeting with Raelin Montrose changes her life in so many ways that Delaney isn't sure that this isn't destiny.

   Raelin Montrose is a practicing Wiccan, and when the ley lines that run under her home tell her that someone is coming, she can't imagine that she was going to solve a mystery and find the love of her life at the same time.

www.shadoepublishing.com

~ *Because a publisher should stand behind their authors~*

FRANKIE

PRUDENCE MACLEOD
IN COLLABORATION WITH
CRYSTIANNA CRAWFORD

Carrie flees from the demons of her present, trying to protect the ones she loves.

Frankie hides from the demons of her past, and the memory of loved ones she failed to protect.

A modern day princess thrown to the wolves, Carrie's only hope is the rancher who had spent the better part of a decade in self imposed, near total, isolation. Frankie's history of losing those she tries to save haunts her, but this madman threatens her home, her livestock, her sanctuary. She knows she can't do it alone, has she still got enough support from her oldest friends?

www.shadoepublishing.com

If you have enjoyed this book and the others listed here Shadoe Publishing is always looking for first, second, or third time authors. Please check out our website @
www.shadoepublishing.com
For information or to contact us @
shadoepublishing@gmail.com.

We may be able to help you make your dreams of becoming a published author come true.

Made in the USA
Columbia, SC
18 May 2019